A Light in the Dunes

For Graeme,

I hope you will
enjoy this story
of great adventures!

Best Wishes
from
martha attena
—

Nov. 16, 2002

A Light
in the Dunes

martha attema

ORCA BOOK PUBLISHERS

To Romkje and Sjoerd but especially to Rikst,
whom we named after the witch of the bird sanctuary.

Canadian Cataloguing in Publication Data
Attema, Martha, 1949 -
A light in the dunes

ISBN 1-55143-085-1
I. Title.
PS8551.T74L53 1997   jC813'.54   C96-910825-7   PZ7.A8864Li
1997

Library of Congress Catalog Card Number: 97-65300

The publisher would like to acknowledge the ongoing financial
support of The Canada Council, the Department of Canadian
Heritage and the British Columbia Ministry of Small Business,
Tourism and Culture.

Cover design by Christine Toller
Cover painting by Ken Campbell
Printed and bound in Canada

Orca Book Publishers   Orca Book Publishers
PO Box 5626, Station B   PO Box 468
Victoria, BC V8R 6S4   Custer, WA 98240-0468
Canada   USA

99 98   5 4 3 2

Acknowledgements

Thanks to the following people, whose assistance and support helped me complete this story:

Marla J. Hayes, Bea Mooney and Wendy Champaign for their encouragement and editorial suggestions; the members of the North Bay Writer's Group and the North Bay Children's Writers' Group for their ongoing support and enthusiam; Donna Sinclair for encouraging me to research the heroines in legends and myths; Albert, Romkje and Sjoerd and Rikst Attema for their moral support; being named after the witch, I owed Rikst for the story. Her courage and determination to overcome the obstacles life has confronted her with, inspired me to complete this novel.

Pronunciation Guide

Rikst de Bruin	rick-st de bréw-in
Bas de Jong	baz de yung
Thomas Scheepstra	tómaz schápe-straw
Nelly de Bruin	néll-ee de bréw-in
Jan de Bruin	yon de bréw-in
Boukje de Bruin	bówk-yah de bréw-in
Marijke Faber	ma-rée-kay fáa-bur
Sjoerd	shóe-ert
Anna	anna
Wietske	véet-ska
Oud	out
Kiewiet	kéy-weet
Piet	peet
Visser	fís-er
Saakje	sák-yeah
Smid	smit

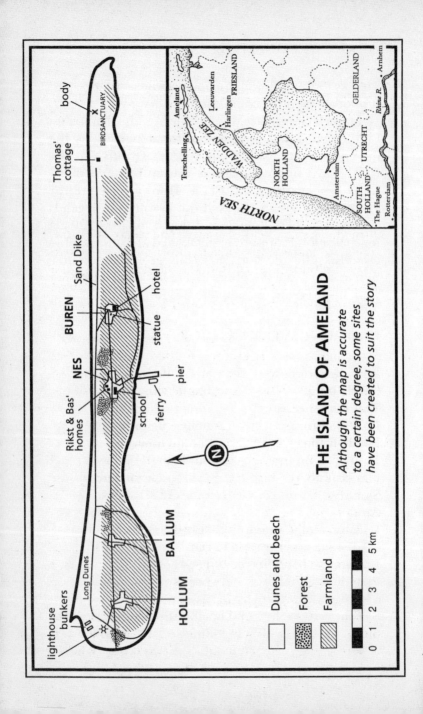

THE ISLAND OF AMELAND

Although the map is accurate to a certain degree, some sites have been created to suit the story

Dunes and beach

Forest

Farmland

0 1 2 3 4 5 km

HOLLUM

BALLUM

NES

BUREN

lighthouse
bunkers

Long Dunes

Rikst & Bas' homes

school

ferry

pier

statue

hotel

Sand Dike

Thomas' cottage

body

BIRDSANCTUARY

NORTH SEA

WADDEN ZEE

Terschelling

Ameland

Leeuwarden

Harlingen FRIESLAND

NORTH HOLLAND

Amsterdam

SOUTH HOLLAND

The Hague

Rotterdam

UTRECHT

GELDERLAND

Rhine R. Arnhem

.1.

Bang! The sound of the steel door shutting booms through my skull. I close my eyes. The musty smell that greets me makes my stomach churn. A wave of dizziness engulfs me. My hands want to hold my head. For a moment I forget they are tied behind my back. Now I feel the rope cutting into my skin. Sounds behind me remind me that I am not alone.

Our captors shove Thomas and me into the cellar of the lighthouse. They are the three strange tourists we've been following for the last two weeks. I wish I could go back to the beginning of that time, knowing what I know now.

The short Asian guy pushes me down the five steps of the small cellar. I fall down on the hard floor.

I hear Thomas right behind me.

The burly, red-headed Irishman with the sinister scar on his unshaven chin forces the old skipper down on the floor next to me.

The woman, whom I've named Ice-woman because of her cold, gray eyes and long, white hair, holds a flashlight in one hand. In the other she carries a revolver. I try to look at her face, but she points the flashlight directly into my eyes. The light temporarily blinds me.

When they'd first grabbed us, the Irishman had hit me on the head with something hard. My head felt as if it were going to explode and I blacked out. When I regained consciousness, I found myself lying in the back of the old brown station wagon that we'd seen the trio driving around the island. Something warm and sticky trickled down behind my ear. With our faces down and our hands tied behind our backs, Thomas and I were held against the floorboards by the Irishman. I recognized his army boots. The doors slammed shut. The engine revved. After a rough ride over uneven terrain the car came to a halt. It was only when they jerked us from the station wagon that I realized where our trip had ended — the lighthouse.

"Give me the rope," the redhead snarls. "Now!"

From his pocket the little man pulls a length of nylon rope.

"We kill first? Yes?" The little man speaks with a strange accent and looks at Ice-woman.

"No!" she snaps. "We don't have time now. We have our business to take care of first. Early tomorrow, when the tide comes in, we'll take them out and toss them in the sea."

Ripples of fear gather in my stomach and rush to my arms and legs.

"Throw them into the North Sea. They'll wash ashore and it will look like a drowning accident." She smiles the coldest smile I have ever seen.

I gasp for air. Kill us! No! I close my eyes. This is it. This is the end. But I haven't even lived my life yet. I'm only fourteen.

With his large hands the Irishman forces me around so that my back is against Thomas'. Together the two men begin winding the rope around us. The floor is hard and cold. My head hurts. My wrists are sore.

In a few minutes they finish their task. Now we're bound together. Back to back. Shoulder to shoulder.

"You stupid idiots." The woman sneers. Her voice clangs hollow in the concrete space. Now, I can see her face clearly. Her eyes shoot cold fire. Her thin lips curve downward at the corners, a look of scorn.

"If our lives weren't on the line, I would laugh at you. An ancient skipper and a little girl playing investigators. But you won't get away with this!" She points the revolver at Thomas' head and then at mine. Cold sweat runs down my spine. My body trembles.

"You thought we didn't see you snooping around the bunkers. You and that boy." She aims her gun at my head again. Never did I imagine my life would end like this!

"And you, old man, following us around at the hotel! Ha!" She laughs in disgust. "Well, we followed you and know exactly where you live and what you were up to." My fears were confirmed; it was not coincidence when their station wagon cruised our street Sunday afternoon and on the night of the *Sunderklazen* ball.

"We will be back. Early in the morning. You won't be able to tell your story to that sluggish police officer. I promise."

"Kill me," Thomas speaks in a strained voice. "Let the girl go."

"So she can tell the story? The little witch?"

It occurs to me that, with her startlingly white hair, she doesn't look like a human being. She's a monster. An animal fearing for her life. Threatened by us.

"You old fool!" Her voice cuts the thick air in the cramped space. "You have even less brains than I thought."

Her laugh reminds me of the sound Jan makes when he scrapes his fingernails across the blackboard during algebra. It gives me goose bumps and makes the hairs on my arms stand on end.

"Let's go, men! We have to get rid of our loot." She turns around and shoos her two accomplices out the door. The snap of the heavy padlock jolts me into reality.

Here we are, Thomas and I bound together in the

pitch-black cellar. This is not a bad dream or a scene from an adventure movie where the bad guys always get caught in the end.

"Rikst," Thomas whispers. "Are you okay?"

"No," my voice cracks. "What are we going to do Thomas? They'll be back and then …"

"Sh. Sh. We're not dead yet."

"But nobody knows we're here."

"I know," Thomas sighs. "We have to think of something."

Thomas squirms on the floor and I have no choice but to move with him.

"I'm sorry I got you into this mess, Thomas."

"It's my own fault. I shouldn't have taken you to the west part of the island."

"No, it was my fault, Thomas. I wanted you to see the grave."

"I should never have listened to you. We should have stayed away from the bunkers. But there's not much we can do about that now."

"Will Piet, the lighthouse guard, check this room?" I ask softly, knowing the answer already.

"I doubt it, Rikst. There's nothing here for him to check. Unless he hears something."

"Do you know what time he goes up the tower?" I try again. With the pain in my head I find it hard to think clearly.

"Even if we knew his schedule, we have no clue what time it is ourselves."

I give up. Thomas' breathing fills the cellar and I try to slow down my own. My throat feels constricted. I'm all choked up. Tears cloud my eyes. I can't give up yet. I have to be strong for Mom and Dad and for my sister, Boukje.

"Thomas?"

"Yes."

"I'm glad Bas isn't with us. Thank goodness he had a dentist appointment this afternoon."

"I wish we'd all had dentist appointments this afternoon. Even though I haven't seen a dentist for over thirty years."

I don't know how to respond. A feeling of guilt washes over me. Now the old skipper is going to die a miserable death in the hands of these thugs and it's my fault.

"I don't want to die, Thomas."

Thomas doesn't answer. I try to calm myself. It doesn't work. To die in a small space like this. Even though I can't see, I feel the walls closing in on me, trapping me like a caged seagull. Maybe I'll die before the crooks come back. Maybe I'll suffocate.

"Thomas? Are you hurt?"

"One of them hit me on the head while I tried to struggle with the Asian guy. I think it was Ice-woman." He leans against me. My body folds.

"If I'm not home at suppertime, Mom will ask Bas if he knows where I am. He'll probably tell them what we've found out. If we're lucky, they'll come looking for us."

"Yes, that's a possibility. But do you think they'll figure out we're in the cellar of the lighthouse?"

"No." My spirits sink. "Wait! Our bikes are parked at the fence."

"Then that's our only hope. The bicycles."

"Thomas?"

"Yes."

"I'm scared."

"I know how you feel," he says.

"You know what the worst part is?" I say in a choking voice, "I didn't get a chance to find out my mom's secret. Why she named me after that horrible woman, the witch of the bird sanctuary!"

"I know," Thomas mumbles.

Then, my thoughts return to a picture. The photograph of a newborn baby. Who was the baby? And why was the picture hidden in the compartment of Mom's antique music box?

The rope cuts into my upper arms. The inside of my head pounds as if the gnomes, who live in the hollow oak tree near the sanctuary, were hard at work with hammers.

I see in my mind the body on the beach, the body of a man Bas and I had found, that stormy Monday afternoon, two weeks ago. A stronger picture replaces the first one — the ghost of Rixt standing on top of the dune, her black cape billowing and her long, white hair blowing in the wind.

Then my world turns black.

.2.

"Hey, Witch," Dirk whispered. "A nice day for beach-combing. Perhaps you'll find a few dead bodies?"

"Oh, you jerk!"

"Will you dress up as the witch of the bird sanctuary on Thursday night?"

I stuck out my tongue. Slamming the door of my locker, I hurried to my Dutch class, his laugh following me through the hallway. I could kill Dirk. Why did he always have to bug me?

When I walked into the room, most of my classmates were already in their seats. I plunked down beside Marijke, who had been my friend since kindergarten. I pulled a black binder and textbook out of my backpack and threw it on my desk. My hair swung in front of my eyes. I scooped it back with my hand.

"My, you're in a fine mood today." Marijke looked at me.

"Sorry, Marijke. I shouldn't let him get to me. That stupid Dirk … "

"Did he tease you again? What did he want this time?"

"Oh, he wanted to know if I will be dressed up as Rixt from the bird sanctuary, for the *Sunderklazen* ball Thursday night."

"Just ignore him," my friend answered. "Is your costume ready?"

"Yes. How about yours? Are you going to tell me what you're going to be?"

Marijke laughed and shook her head. "Not until we meet Thursday night."

"Good morning, class," Miss Oud, our grade eight teacher, walked in, cheery as always. With her gray hair tied in the traditional bun, she wore a pink mohair sweater with matching skirt. Looking over her bifocals, she peered around the classroom. Her eyes rested on me, as she continued, "I'll start with some exciting news. The school received the information for the Dutch short story contest. Rikst, sit up straight!"

Quickly, I straightened my back.

In the same breath Miss Oud continued, "This year's theme is the history of your area."

"How boring," Marijke whispered.

"This doesn't mean you're confined to using just historical facts," Miss Oud added, "You can take any event or character from the past and use this for your story. For your research you can use the library and the various museums. We also have some seniors on the island who wouldn't mind being interviewed."

Her eyes still were on me, so I didn't move. I pretended to listen intently. Miss Oud was strict and old-fashioned, but I liked her, even though she picked on kids like me who had a hard time sitting still in these uncomfortable desks. The desks were built for people with short legs. My long limbs started cramping after five minutes and I had to squirm around. I couldn't help myself.

"To make your short story interesting, you take the truth and stretch it. The story is due Friday, December 12th and will count for thirty percent of your final mark. The two winners will be announced December 17th. That's a Wednesday. And, of course, the winners' stories will be entered in the National competition. Any questions?"

"Don't you agree that Rikst should write about the witch of the bird sanctuary?" Dirk had raised his arm.

"The nerve of that guy," I hissed at Marijke.

Dirk sat at the front of the room. I glared at him. Sure, he is tall, handsome, with dark, curly hair and brown eyes, but he knows it too well. Look at that smug face. Why do most girls in my class have a crush on him? Even Marijke adores him. I just hate the guy. He's arrogant and has a big mouth. Just because his dad owns the two ferry boats doesn't make him king of the island. Lately he's found pleasure in teasing me about my name and the woman my parents named me after– the witch of the bird sanctuary.

I don't seem to share the same ideas and hobbies as the other girls. It's just me and Marijke; the rest of the group follow Linda. She's the mayor's daughter and bosses everyone around. They copy her hair style and wear the same brand-name clothes but their main hobby is boys. I refuse to dress like everyone else and I'm not interested in boys the way they are.

"Who or what will you write about?" Marijke cut into my thoughts.

"I don't know," I shrugged. Miss Oud finally took her eyes off me. "My mom might have some information at the museum."

"Can I come with you? Your mom won't mind, will she?" my friend asked.

"Of course not. She loves to talk about the history of the island. If she works Wednesday, we can go after school."

Miss Oud talked about a test, but my mind wandered off. The wind howled and beat at the tiles on the roof. A great storm was roaring in from the northwest which meant the sea would throw its wares up on the beach.

I wondered if Bas would come with me after school.

Bas and his mother live next door to us. They are practically part of our family; we do everything together. Bas is only five months older than I, but he's in the other grade eight class in the school.

Most kids my age on Ameland go to the grade seven and eight classes in the town of Nes, where I live. Some go to high schools on the mainland after grade seven, but most, like my sister Boukje, who is sixteen, attend the high schools after completing grade eight.

"You're not still steaming about Dirk, are you?" Marijke said.

"Are you kidding? I don't care what he says. What test was Miss Oud talking about?"

•••

The storm roared all day and when the last bell rang I hurried to my locker and took out my coat.

"No running in the hall, Witch! Those bodies won't dash away!" Dirk sneered at me.

As I ran home, I clenched my fists. It made me so angry sometimes! Why did my parents have to name me after Rixt of the bird sanctuary — Rixt, the witch of one of our island's many legends. Ever since the town of Buren had raised a statue in memory of Rixt, I had been teased at school. Naturally the monument didn't portray her as a pretty lady. She looks like an old hag, her back bent, leaning on a stick, her weathered face and scrawny body covered in rags.

Why Dirk compares me with the statue is a mystery to me. I'm tall, the tallest girl in my class by far, taller, in fact than all the boys except Dirk. My long arms and legs sometimes make me feel a bit like an octopus. My hair is straight, long and blond, and freckles are scattered all over my nose and cheekbones.

"Hi, Mom!"

Mom walked down the path to our house. I watched

her and was reminded again how different we are. Mom is of only average height and has dark blond, curly hair. People say I'm a replica of my dad. Boukje looks more like Mom. She turned around. It sometimes seems that Mom hardly ever smiles. Her facial expressions are somber. We do not always see eye to eye, Mom and I. She blames it on my hormones. But I think Mom should take life a little less seriously and not make a big deal out of every little issue.

"Are you early today?" she asks.

I slowed down to catch my breath. "I ran most the way. Is Bas home?"

"Haven't seen him yet. Are you and Bas going to the beach tonight?"

"Yes. As soon as he's ready."

"What about your homework?" Mom said as she opened the front door.

"Don't worry, Mom. I'll do it later. Are you working this Wednesday?"

"Yes. Why?"

"Marijke and I want to come to the museum to do some research for the short story contest." In the hallway I kicked off my shoes and hung up my rain coat.

"What's the topic this year?" Mom asked from the kitchen as she plugged in the kettle for tea.

"The history of our area. Miss Oud said we could choose any event or character from the past."

"Have Marijke and you decided what you'll write about?" Mom cut three thick slices of spice cake and spread them with butter.

"No, that's why we want to look at some things at the museum."

Mom's hands stopped. "There is an interesting legend you could write about, Rikst, but …"

"No! Don't even think it!" My voice sounded harsher than I meant it to. "I know perfectly well what you want me to write about. There were more suggestions like that at school. I WILL NOT WRITE ABOUT RIXT, THE WITCH FROM THE BIRD SANCTUARY!!!!"

"Sorry, Rikst. I didn't mean to upset you. Lately, you've been unhappy with your name and I thought if you did … Here, drink your tea. I think I hear Bas at the back door."

I drank my tea and with trembling fingers broke a piece off the cake, still bristling. Why did Mom have to come up with the same idea everybody else had? How could she expect me to write about the witch? Well, I'm NOT going to.

"Why did you and Dad name me after that terrible woman, anyway?" I looked intently at my mother.

Her face colored. Red patches grew on her high cheekbones and her neck. She put down the knife. Her eyes grew distant. For a moment I thought she'd answer my question. No words came. Then, she continued slicing the cake. She was saved from an answer when the kitchen door opened.

"Hi, Rikst. Are you ready to go? Hi, Aunt Nel."

"You want tea, Bas?"

"No, thanks, but I would like a piece of cake."

While Bas ate his cake, I changed into some old clothes.

"Don't be too long, Rikst. We still have to work on your costume for the ball."

"No, we won't be late. Bye, Mom."

We took our bikes and headed off.

In town we were sheltered by the houses and didn't feel the strong wind too much. With the wind behind us, we left Nes and sailed to the next little town of Buren. From that point on the wind blew from the side. It took great effort to stay on the road. Bas rode in front of me, his back bent, his arms flat on the handle bars. It was easier for Bas; he isn't as tall as I am. I followed closely. We didn't talk much. As we passed the statue of Rixt, I looked at it. Yes, she does look like an old hag with her ragged clothes and cantankerous face.

"Come on, Rikst!" Bas shouted.

I could hardly hear him. The wind roared like mad and I had to pedal hard to keep up. After we passed the campground, I found it almost impossible to stay on the bike.

"Isn't this great weather?!" Bas screamed.

"Yes. There will be lots of stuff on the beach!!" I yelled back.

Once we were on Sand Dike it became easier to pedal. Again the wind pushed us in the back, as we bicycled all the way to the bird sanctuary. Here the path ended. Carrying our bikes, we climbed over the dune. In the shelter of the dunes rests a small cottage. First, the pointed top of the thatched roof came in sight. We walked down to the weathered, wooden gate and parked our bikes against it.

"You think he's home?" I asked.

"Knowing him, he's probably already at the beach."

Nobody answered as Bas rang the ship's bell beside the green door.

"He's gone," Bas said and nodded his head in the direction of the sea.

We climbed over the gate and onto the next dune. On top we stopped. I tugged at Bas' jacket and pointed at the sea. Beneath us lay the beach. The sea roared and waves crashed onto the sand. The breakers looked as high as houses. How small and insignificant I felt compared to the force of nature. The wind gusted, a giant's breath trying to blow us off the dune.

We surveyed the shoreline to the east as far as the island stretched. Then, we scanned westward. The beach seemed abandoned except for three black-headed gulls struggling, like us, with the forces of nature.

"He isn't here!" I yelled at Bas.

"Maybe he went to town!!"

"Let's go!!"

We tumbled down the dune and walked down to the shore. The tide, now receding, had left behind some of its mysteries.

When we were seven, Dad had begun taking Bas and me to the beach after heavy storms. He'd shown us the best places to find the treasures that the sea gave up. Ever since that time, Bas and I had become the island's youngest beachcombers. Some of the kids at school made fun of us, as if we were doing something alien. But years ago lots of people on the island had made a living from beachcombing. Nowadays, however, it seemed that only old fishermen and the odd tourist searched the beaches after storms.

The first thing that caught my eye was a bottle. I picked it up and wiped the sand away with my sleeve. A long, slim neck and a short, round belly gave the bottle an unusual shape. The green glass was textured with little bumps.

"That's a beauty for your collection!" Bas said.

The thunder of the waves accompanied us as we walked eastward on the beach. But at least the wind was mostly at our backs. Bas picked up a piece of driftwood and carried it under his arm. Now and then we stopped to look at an old crate, a barrel or a box. When we were little, we always fantasized about finding a treasure chest full of gold from a pirate ship.

Monstrous black clouds moved in from behind us. The first raindrops hit the sand.

"Let's go back and see if Thomas is home!!" Bas screamed.

As I turned, my eyes spotted something farther up the beach. I swiveled back and pointed in the direction of a heap in the sand. Bas followed my gaze.

"Let's check it out!!" he hollered. He took my hand. We ran about a hundred meters. Suddenly, we stopped. Whatever lay in the sand perhaps forty meters down the beach was a brownish color. I looked at Bas. He squinted at the mound.

"It looks like a body!" I shouted above the roar of the waves.

Bas nodded. One step at a time we moved closer. Tension crept from my neck into arms and legs. A tight crampy feeling filled my stomach. My eyes were glued to the form. It could also be a sack of some kind, or a bale of fabric, or …

Time seemed to have slowed. The roar of the storm now seemed to come from a long way off. But finally we stood next to the the focus of our curiosity. I found it difficult to swallow as I stared at the brown shape in the sand.

It WAS a body. Sweat broke out of every pore on my skin. I'd never seen a dead person before. Covered with sand and strings of seaweed, a man lay face down, one arm flung to one side, the other twisted awkwardly at the shoulder. His hair was short and a reddish blond. He wore a green rain slicker and slacks. His right foot was stuck in a brown rubber boot. The other foot was bare. The tide must have carried him in and smashed him onto the beach.

I looked at Bas' face. His skin color had changed to gray.

"Are you all right?" I asked when I found my voice.

He shook his head and turned away. He stumbled a few feet away from the body, fell on his knees and threw up. I quickly looked away, fighting hard to gain control of my own stomach.

I gazed far out into the North Sea. Not one ship outlined the horizon. I scanned the beach both ways. There was nobody. Not a soul walked on the entire beach. Then I turned my head in the direction of the dunes. I froze. A raw cry drowned by the thunder of the breakers broke from my throat. There, on top of the dune stood a woman. She wore a long, billowing cloak. Her white hair blew in the wind.

"Rixt! Bas! It's the ghost of Rixt!"

I tried to scream, but no sound emerged. Had time turned around, and taken me back two hundred years to a time when an old woman stood on top of the dunes during heavy storms, waiting for her prey?

I turned to look at Bas. He was still on his knees, head bent to the sand. My eyes surveyed the dunes again. The apparition was gone. Once more I looked. My gaze returned to the body and from the body to Bas, who slowly rose to his feet. His face was as pale as the sand.

Rixt? Did I see the ghost of Rixt, the witch of the bird sanctuary? No. Was it an apparition? My imagination?

"Perhaps you'll find a few dead bodies." Dirk's nasty words echoed in my mind.

"We have to tell Thomas and go to the police!" Bas shouted.

Numb all over, I only nodded.

"What's wrong?" The color was returning to Bas' face. "Are you OK? You look like you've seen a ghost."

Again I nodded. Bas shook his head. He pulled the strings of his hood in a tight knot and grabbed my hand. We started running. We now faced the wind head on. It tried to force us back and blew my hair straight out behind me. Just like the witch, I thought. Just like the woman I'd just seen on the dunes. Or had I?

We kept on running. I stumbled, hobbling half behind Bas, who tried to hold me upright. I no longer heard the sea's angry roars, nor did I smell her saltiness. I didn't even feel the wind pushing me back. All I saw was the body in the sand and the woman standing on top of the dune.

.3.

Out of breath I followed Bas to the door of the skipper's cottage.

"Thomas! Thomas!"

As if expecting us, the door opened before we could knock.

"Hey, guys, slow down. Come in. I'll make you some cranberry tea."

"No, Thomas," I gasped. "We have to go to the police. There's a body on the beach. And I saw Rixt!"

"You saw Rixt when we were out there," Bas' mouth fell open. "But …"

"Yes, I saw the witch when you were vomiting! But I knew you wouldn't believe me!"

We followed Thomas inside the small cottage. He pointed to a chair. I let myself fall onto it. Swallowing back my tears, I looked out the window. A seagull rested on one of the fence poles. Oh, why did I get upset? I took a deep breath. The warmth and comfort of the cozy kitchen slowly replaced the coldness and fear that we'd brought in from the beach.

The kettle on the woodstove in the corner whistled softly.

"We do believe you, Rikst," Thomas said in a calm voice. "But before we go to the police, I want you to tell me where you found the body and where you saw the ghost of Rixt. One night I …" Thomas blinked. "Others have seen Rixt wandering through the dunes in weather like this. Her ghost is very much alive."

As Bas recounted what had happened, I watched the old skipper. Thomas' face frowned as he listened to Bas. The silver, white hair that framed his bony face was in dire need of a cut. His tanned skin was as lined and cracked as worn leather. His eyes, sometimes dark and ominous, sometimes sparkling, always brightened his face. A white mustache covered his upper lip. He wore a blue, knitted sweater with a large hole at the elbow.

Thomas had lived such an interesting life. Until a couple of years ago he had been the captain of a cargo boat. He'd travelled to every seaport in the world. After his retirement, he'd built this cottage on a small parcel of land on the edge of the bird sanctuary. He'd become a conservationist, actively involved in environmental committees and action groups to protect what little nature we have left on the island.

Thomas' home looked more like a ship's galley than a house. At the back, the windows were portholes. The walls in the living room were covered with artifacts from far away countries. Two whale jawbones, souvenirs of his early years on the whaling ships, formed an archway at the entrance to the cottage. A heavily rusted anchor sat in the front yard.

When I had once asked him why he didn't live in one of the small towns on the island, Thomas explained, "The sea has always been my home and I don't want to spend the rest of my life away from it." The only family he had was an older brother who lived in a home for senior citizens in Nes. Thomas had been a family friend for as long as I could remember.

"Let's go back to the place you found the body and then I'll come with you to the police station." Thomas got up and grabbed his oil slicker from a hook in the corner.

We didn't say much as we climbed over the dunes to the beach. The three of us plodded through sand and rubble in the direction of the body.

When the wind slapped my hair in my face, I tightened the string of my hood and tucked my hair inside. I wondered if I had been hallucinating when I saw the woman standing on top of the dune. I pushed the thought away and focused on the dead body. Had the man fallen off a ship? Had someone deliberately knocked him overboard?

"Wasn't it here, Rikst?" Bas interrupted my thoughts.

"Yes, I think so," I answered. "Or maybe a little further."

"No, it was here," Bas said. "There's where I got sick. It was right here!" he said again.

The sand was covered with footprints where the body had lain. But other than that there was no evidence that anything had ever been there. The body was gone. It had disappeared. Vanished. Like it was all a bad dream. I rubbed my eyes and looked around again.

My bottle and Bas' piece of driftwood lay in the sand close to where we'd found the corpse.

"Let's follow the footprints," I suggested.

"Which footprints?" Thomas asked. "There are so many."

I scanned the sea, the beach and the dunes. There still wasn't a ship in sight. Thomas and Bas copied my actions.

"What do we do now?" Bas yelled above the roar of the wind. "I'd feel pretty stupid going to the police to report a body that has disappeared. Officer Kiewiet wouldn't believe us!"

"We must still tell him!" Thomas yelled. "He might have a list of missing persons."

Back at Thomas' cottage, we discussed how and what we would tell the police. The old skipper wanted to come with us, but not until we drank his famous cranberry tea and ate a raisin bun spread with a thick layer of butter.

It was getting late as the three of us pedaled back to Nes. Officer Kiewiet, our friendly, round-faced policeman, invited us into his office in the island's only police station.

"What can I do for you?" He touched his fingers to his cap.

We sat down and told our story. Then the officer started his questioning. What time had we found the body? Where exactly had we found it? What did the body look like? How was it dressed?

I wasn't sure if I should mention the woman in the dunes and decided not to. I couldn't see how a ghost would have anything to do with the dead person unless she had taken it away. The appearance of Rixt could be my imagination playing tricks on me. Besides, she couldn't carry a body. At least, I didn't think so. I was no longer sure exactly what I'd seen.

Officer Kiewiet promised to look into the matter and check on missing people. He would get back to Thomas.

"Did he take us seriously?" Bas asked, as we picked up our bikes.

"We'll wait and see if he gets in touch with me," Thomas answered. "I'll let you know. Say hi to your parents. I'll come by for Saint Nicholas Eve.

Dinner was already on the table and Mom and Dad were about to begin eating when I got home.

"I see you found another one of my favorite sweaters," Dad smiled. Mom gave me a look of disapproval for wearing Dad's oversized, black sweater. She wants me to look more like a girl, but I prefer clothes I can live in. Except for the sleeves, which I have to roll up several times, Dad's clothes are just so comfortable.

"It's like wearing a dress with jeans," Mom sighed. "And the styles are so feminine this season. Not that I would approve of you borrowing my clothes, like Boukje used to do, but at least you wouldn't be dressed like a hobo."

"Any real treasures on the beach, Rikst?" Dad changed the subject.

I swallowed. "Yes, I found this interesting bottle for my collection and, and, we found a body."

"A body!" Mom's eyes opened wide. She almost dropped a platter of meat. "You mean a real human body? We must go to the police immediately."

"We already went," I said. "But then it was gone."

"What? The body had disappeared?" Dad said.

I told them how, after finding the body, Bas and I had gone to Thomas' cottage and when we returned, all signs of the dead man had vanished.

"Perhaps it washed back into the sea," Mom said. "I don't like you wandering on the beach when there are bodies lying around!"

"No, Mom, the tide was going out. The waves didn't even come close to where we discovered it. And normally there are no dead people on the beach."

"That's very strange indeed," Dad said. "Perhaps Officer Kiewiet will find out if someone went missing. At the office today I heard the coast guard report on the radio, and I don't think they mentioned any boating accidents."

We ate the rest of our meal in silence. I thought about Rixt again. Why was I named after this woman? If she had done something good for the island, it would have been an honor to be named after her. But this woman had been a witch who'd roamed the beaches and took everything the sea left behind. The legend said she had even tricked ships by signaling them with a light in the dunes, so big boats would run aground.

Then, she would rob them of their cargo. I decided that for now I would keep her appearance to myself.

After supper I tried on my costume for the ball on Thursday. On our island we still follow the old tradition of the *Sunderklazen*. This is the celebration surrounding the birthday of Saint Nicholas. Dad had found the neatest troll heads in a joke shop on the mainland last year. When he brought them home, Mom had called him crazy. But a few weeks ago Mom and I decided that the heads would be perfect for a two-headed troll costume. In one of the heads we'd made holes for my eyes, nose and mouth. The other head was sewn onto the shoulder of a fake fur costume in brown and orange colors. Mom was sewing big black claws on the sleeves. We couldn't decide if I should wear Dad's boots or if we should sew claws that cover my shoes. The last idea might be more comfortable, but was more work for my mother. My sewing skills are pitiful.

"All right," Mom sighed. "I'll cut out the pattern from the black fur and sew elastic on either side, so you can slip the claws over your shoes. And now you better go up to your room to do homework."

"Yes, Mom. Thanks for the claws."

Upstairs, I added the green bottle to my collection. Dad had built me a large shelving unit for my bottles last winter.

I sat down at my desk and stared out the window. Unfortunately, I couldn't see the sea or the dunes, only the neighbor's yard. But I liked my room at the back of the house. Boukje, my sister, had her room at the front. Her room was much noisier than mine because it was on the street side.

Besides the shelving unit and desk, I owned an antique oak bed and matching night table from my grandparents, two rattan chairs and a small table and a dresser. I loved the smell of the Chinese mats on my floor. Mom had made curtains, pillows and a bedspread out of rose cotton fabric.

Two seagulls carved out of driftwood stood on my dresser. After Bas collected the driftwood, he carved birds and small animals. The two on my dresser were gifts from him.

On the wall above my bed hung three enlarged photographs mounted onto posterboard: one of the dunes and the lighthouse, one of the breakers and one of a lonely seagull. Boukje had become a talented photographer in the last few years. Every Friday Boukje came home from the high school on the mainland. I was glad she could come home every weekend. We used to fight a lot, but now that she wasn't around during the week, we got along quite well. It was quiet without her.

In September, I would be going to the high school there, too. Looking at the photographs two things came to mind. I would miss the island and the sea terribly. And I didn't think I'd like living in the city.

I checked my homework. Besides math, I didn't have much. Opening the top drawer, my hand reached for a small book. Ever since Marijke gave it to me for my tenth birthday, I have written my inner thoughts in this book of secrets. Bound in burgundy leather, the diary had a small gold-etched rose in the bottom corner.

Monday, December 1

Dear Friend,

Today was an eventful day. Dirk teased me again and I don't know why I got so upset. Marijke said I should ignore him and she is right. You, my friend, would probably agree with her.

There was a great storm. The wind-whipped breakers reached at least five meters before they came crashing down. You should have heard their maddening, thundering sound. We found the body of a man on the beach. It was sinister!! Bas couldn't handle it and puked in the sand.

We ran to find Thomas, but when the three of us returned, the body had disappeared. The weirdest thing of all was the appearance of a woman on top of the dunes. (At first I was sure it was Rixt!) Her long cloak billowed in the wind. Her straight, white hair blew in front of her. Bas didn't see her. And there was nobody else on the beach. I was afraid my imagination had taken over. Do you believe I was hallucinating? I didn't think Bas and Thomas would believe me, but Thomas said I wasn't the only one who had seen the ghost of Rixt during this kind of weather. Now I am not so sure what it was I saw. Did I really see the woman or was it my imagination? Was it an omen?

Then there's the short story contest. Bas suggested I research the legend of Rixt, find all the different versions that have been written about her life and then make my own. I don't know. I vowed I wouldn't write about her. Just because Mom and Dirk had suggested it. But I have to admit she's never far from my mind. The legend intrigues me. What do you think, my dear friend? Should I be proud and stubborn or should I give in and find out?

I still haven't found out why I was named after the witch. I asked again, but, as always, Mom avoided answering. But I swear to you I will not rest until I find out why I was named after a woman who lured ships in the night. Mom can't or won't talk about it. But I won't give up. This is my quest. I need to know. You probably think I'm stubborn and perhaps you are right.

Wednesday I'll decide on the topic of my short story, when Marijke and I go to the museum. Who knows, I might find another intriguing character. I'll let you know.

My costume for the Sunderklazen ball is turning out great. I will have some great claws and if I can find out what Dirk is going to be, those claws might come in handy.

Good night, friend.

After locking my diary, I placed it back in my top drawer. In my backpack I found my math book. I finished the questions and went downstairs.

I could hear the sewing machine running in the kitchen. Mom was still working on my costume. It took a lot of patience. I walked into the dining room. His tall body bent, Dad was pouring over some drawings at the table. A lock of straight, blond hair covered his forehead.

Dad's always so relaxed about everything. Perhaps I should ask him about my name instead of Mom. It's much easier to talk to him. Whenever we touch on a subject she isn't comfortable with, Mom erects an invisible wall around herself. Dad is much more approachable, but now was not a good time. I went over and tried to figure out what all the lines on his drawing meant. Dad works as an engineer for the Ministry of Waterways and Public Works.

"We are losing the west side of the island to the sea." Dad pointed at the drawing. "We need to do something soon or we'll lose another part of the dunes. The sea is powerful and takes away land from one side of the island, while on the south side the sea gives us land. During the storm today, the dune close to the lighthouse was partially washed away. You and Bas should have a look this week."

"Maybe tomorrow afternoon," I answered. "I still have to do some last minute shopping for Saint Nicholas Eve." I still get excited about the evening of the fifth of December when people in the Netherlands and Belgium exchange gifts to celebrate the birthday of Saint Nicholas.

"I still need a gift for Mom," Dad whispered. "I saw this book about antique china in the bookstore in Ballum. Do you think she would like that?"

"Yes. She would love it, especially now that she's starting a collection of antique teapots."

"I'll buy it tomorrow. And Rikst, will you help me write the poem?" Dad made a sad face. "You know those *Sinterklaas* poems are a nightmare for me to write. My brain has never been good at rhyming."

I could never resist his dog-starving-for-attention face. "Sure, Dad. You're lucky I have finished all my poems and wrapped my gifts."

"I need some help with the wrapping, too," he added.

I smiled and turned on the television. I flicked the channels, but there was nothing interesting on that night. Instead, I found a book on the history of the dikes. While reading, my thoughts wandered to the woman with flying white hair and a dark cloak.

.4.

The next day after school Bas and I biked to Hollum, the town at the west end of the island. Although still brisk, the wind had calmed down quite a bit. We took the road from Nes to the small town of Ballum, where we stopped at a jewellery store because I still needed to buy Marijke a present. I found a neat pair of sterling silver earrings. Each earring contained three dangling stars. Bas found a sculptured clay brooch in abstract shapes painted blue and brown for his mom. We left the store with our gifts and pedaled north through the Long Dunes.

West of Hollum stands the lighthouse, tall and straight as a giant guard. We parked our bikes there and walked to the beach. The damage done by the storm was incredible. One third of the dune was gone, swept away by high waves.

"I can't believe it," Bas said. "Today the sea acts as if nothing has happened. Look how gently the waves are rolling onto the beach."

I could hear the breakers. They made a deep continuous rumble. The anger of the storm had left them.

"It's fascinating, the strength nature has," I answered. "The sea will never allow us to control her. Once in a while she lets us know who has the power."

We walked down the shoreline and I picked up some shells. This was where I liked to be, close to the sea, surrendering myself to her ever-changing moods. Some days, like Monday, she showed her anger and her power; today she wanted to please, calm us. Bas crouched down and stared out over the water at an oil tanker chugging slowly across the horizon. I watched the seagulls dive into the waves. Every time one bird caught a fish, the others swooped down and tried to steal it.

We walked north to the end of the island. I don't really like this area of the dunes, which is still littered with barbed wire fencing from the Second World War. Dad had explained that the German occupants had built their bunkers in the dunes as part of the Atlantic Wall defence system. From the bunkers cannons would fire at allied boats that came too close to shore as they passed through the North Sea on their way to England. Nazi anti-aircraft guns were also aimed at bombers flying to missions in Germany. Big signs on the fence around the bunkers read KEEP OUT!! and DANGER!!

The walls and roof of the bunkers were made of concrete a meter thick. Two heavy, steel doors closed the front entrance. A smaller escape door was at the back. The bunkers were mostly hidden from view by sand and bush. I often wished the government would destroy the bunkers and restore the dunes to their natural state. As it was now this whole area felt like a forbidden zone. Its violent history didn't belong in this peaceful conservation area.

Two bunkers were located at this end of the island. As we walked past the first one, I stopped. A shiver ran down my spine.

"We are being watched," I said. "From behind the second bunker."

"I don't see anything," Bas peered in the direction I had mentioned.

I looked again. Although I was unable to explain what I had seen, I'd felt the presence of something or somebody. It was hard to tell if someone was really out there. The dune was covered with marram grass and wild rose bushes.

"Let's go back, Bas. This place gives me the creeps," I said.

"It's time to head home anyway." Bas looked at his watch.

We picked up our bikes at the lighthouse gate. Pretty soon the automatic light would come on. The powerful rays would sweep over land and sea at intervals of three seconds, rotating uninterrupted all through the night. Ships could see those lights from a great distance.

I looked up at the glass dome where the light would glow.

"Did you want a look inside?" Piet, the lighthouse guardsman, walked up to the tower.

"Do we have time?" I asked Bas. He nodded and we leaned our bicycles back against the fence.

"Quite a storm, yesterday," Piet said as he unlocked the door and let us in. We entered a small hallway with a steep, narrow staircase leading up to the top. Across from the stairs was another door secured by a padlock. A sign on the door read "KEEP OUT."

"Did you see the part we lost on Monday? If we don't do something soon, by the time the next storm shows up, the lighthouse might be gone."

"My dad's working on it," I said as I climbed the stairs behind Bas and the guard.

"Yes, I saw him," the guard answered.

"He was here yesterday to check the dunes," I added.

"As long as they don't study the project too long. The sea doesn't wait."

I forgot to count, but there were many steps before we finally reached the top. Piet opened the door to the glass dome. We walked around the many lenses that reflect the light.

"Yesterday, I couldn't see very far, but today you can see the mainland, the island of Terschelling and far over the North Sea," Piet said.

"There are the two drilling rigs." Bas pointed to the east. I followed his gaze and saw the giant platforms sticking high above the waves.

"I'm glad I wasn't on one of those yesterday during the storm," Piet said.

I looked at Bas. His face turned dark. When Bas was only three, his father, who had worked on one of the platforms, had drowned during a storm. Bas never talked about his father, but I knew he was thinking about him now.

To the west I saw the island of Terschelling. Two years ago, we visited there. That island is much bigger than the one we're on. Ameland is only twenty-seven kilometers long and its width ranges from about two to four kilometers. The island has only four small villages. My eyes scanned the north side of our island, where lie the dunes, the beaches and the forests. Farmland, gained from sea clay, makes up the southern part of the island.

The eastern part of Ameland is a conservation area and bird sanctuary. The northwest part of the island, where the lighthouse is, is a protected area as well. Here many animals and birds can live and breed undisturbed. These two areas are patrolled in the summertime when the island is invaded by tourists.

"It must be kind of quiet up here at this time of year," I said.

"Usually it is," Piet replied. "But today I've actually had other visitors. Some strange tourists. Two men and a woman. Two of them spoke English with a heavy Irish or Scottish accent. The third one looked Asian. He didn't talk much. The woman had long, white hair and wore sunglasses. It was hard to tell if her bleached hair was real or a wig. They seemed interested in the bunkers. I tried to explain that the shelters were sealed off, but I don't speak English very well, so I don't know if they understood what I said."

I swallowed and looked at Bas. A woman with long, white hair. I couldn't believe it. Perhaps it had been the same woman who'd appeared on top of the dune. Was she a tourist? Did she have something to do with the disappearance of the body?

"Did she look like Rixt from the bird sanctuary?" Bas asked.

"No, not at all," Piet laughed. "Rixt's an old hag. This one sure wasn't. She must have been in her late twenties, maybe. Although, she could have been older. It was hard to tell with her sunglasses."

Slowly, the sun sank into the sea; an orange ball falling off the end of the earth. We watched the light in the lighthouse switch on automatically and start its pattern.

"It's all computerized these days," Piet continued.

I didn't listen. "We'd better go, Bas," I said. Bas' mother worried when Bas didn't come home in time for dinner.

I don't remember walking down the stairs. Before I realized it, we were on our bikes. This time we took the main road. When a brown station wagon passed us at full speed, I thought I saw three people in the car, but it was almost too dark to see them clearly. People who live on the island drive within the speed limit, but this car was driving much faster.

I caught up with Bas.

"What do you think, Bas? About the woman?"

"I think you saw the woman Piet described, instead of the ghost of Rixt."

I nodded, but I still had my doubts.

It was rather late when we returned home.

"I hope your mom isn't worried," I said when I stopped in my driveway.

Bas shook his head.

"Are you going out Thursday night?" I asked. Every year on December the fourth we celebrate the evening of the Young Klazes. Between five and eight o'clock in the evening, young men between the ages of twelve and eighteen rule the streets. The boys dress up in white sheets with holes cut out for their eyes. They are so-called "sweepers." They clear the streets of women and children. To scare their victims, they carry decorated sticks and blow their horns. According to tradition, all children and women have to stay inside during this time. Those who disregard the rules risk being beaten up. For young girls, of course, it's exciting to break these rules, and so we would go out into the streets, making sure not to get caught. This tradition dated from the time when people were superstitious and believed in exorcism. On the mainland, the ritual had long vanished. Here on the island, though, people stuck to traditions.

"It's a stupid tradition and discriminates against women," I said.

"Oh, come on, Rikst. That's what it used to be. Now, it's just fun! I'll be one of the sweepers who keeps you off the streets. Will you be out breaking the rules?"

"Of course," I laughed. "Good night, Bas."

After watching Bas ride off, I put my bike away in the shed.

"Dad's late tonight," Mom said. "It's just you and me for dinner. And your costume is finished."

"Oh, great. I'll try it on after supper."

During our meal I told Mom about the lighthouse and the foreign tourists. I decided to tell her about the strange appearance in the dunes yesterday.

"It sounds like something from a horror movie. I

hope you won't start investigating on your own, Rikst. Just leave it up to the police."

Of course, I wouldn't investigate. Although I thought about it a lot. I was tempted to find out more but I had no idea how.

"Mom, why did you and Dad name me after Rixt? She was a terrible woman. Why was Boukje named after Grandma and you named me after some witch?" My words rushed out in one long breath.

"Your dad and I never expected the name would make you unhappy. When you're eighteen, you can always change it to whatever you like," Mom answered.

"Isn't that expensive?"

"I don't really know how much that would cost. We can get the information from city hall."

"You did it again, Mom!" My hands clenched together in my lap.

"What?"

"You didn't answer my question. Why did you name me after a witch?"

"We changed the spelling. I never liked the x before the t."

"That's not my question!" The frustration I felt suddenly welled up in me like a huge wave. I stood up, shoved my chair under the table and ran to my room. I didn't bother turning on the lights. I slammed the door so hard the window trembled, and I fell on the bed.

What was it with this name? Why didn't they follow our tradition and name me after Grandma Wietske, just like they had named Boukje after my other grandmother?

Did I really want to change my name? And wait four years until I was eighteen? No, I didn't. All I wanted to know was WHY I was named after a witch. It hadn't even bothered me until they'd built the stupid statue and the teasing had begun. Or did it bother me because I liked storms just like Rixt did?

I loved going down to the beach looking for things. But so did my dad and Bas. I was a beachcomber just like Rixt. But I didn't lure any ships to the beach in the night. Why wouldn't they tell me? It almost seemed as though they had a secret reason not to tell. But I had a right to know! I threw my pillow across the room. It hit the door.

I lay on the bed and stared into the darkness. It seemed to comfort me. My homework stayed in my backpack. I was too angry to think about anything else.

At eleven, I heard Dad come home. I didn't go downstairs to say good night. It took me a long time to fall asleep.

.5.

The Museum of Beachcombing was located in an old
farm on the south side of Buren. Most of its artifacts
had been found on the beach. Parts of ships, crates,
barrels and boxes were set up along the barn walls.
Among these items we saw chairs and tables from Rus-
sia and Finland, vases from China and tea crates from
East Asia.

Marijke and I perused the treasures. It was amazing
how many ceramic and glass items had survived their
long journeys without any damage.

"I still don't know what I'm looking for," Marijke
sounded desperate. Mom came over to help us out.
Mom and I were talking to each other again, no long
conversations, just the bare minimum of necessary information.

"Would you be interested in writing about the castle
of the Cammingha family?" my mother asked. "The lady
of Doniah, who's first name was also Rixt, was called
the mother of the island. She did some significant charity work and she was well-liked. The castle was torn down
in 1829. You can find all the information in the library.
There isn't much here in the museum."

I listened with astonishment. I wanted to scream.
Why wasn't I named after a lady who was respected, but
I bit my tongue. Marijke wasn't aware of the tension
between Mom and me and I didn't feel like explain-

ing. I glared at my mother instead.

Mom turned away, her face flushed, but she was saved by the phone.

Marijke liked the idea about the castle. "That's a great idea. Thanks, Mrs. de Bruin."

"Yes," I said. "It sounds like a wonderful idea."

Some cups and saucers, a few bottles, an oil lamp and a stove was all that was left of Rixt's cottage. I probably would find all the information in the library too.

"Will you come to the library with me, Rikst?"

I nodded.

"Bye, Mom." My voice sounded low.

"Bye, Mrs. de Bruin." We left the museum and biked to Nes to the public library.

"Are you and your mom having a fight?"

"Yes," I shrugged my shoulders. "It's about my name."

"And only because Dirk has been teasing you," Marijke jumped off her bike.

"Yes," I nodded. "Don't you think I have a right to know why I was named after that witch?"

Marijke stared at me with her big brown eyes. "Are you sure you were named after the witch and not after the lady Rixt?"

"I'm one hundred percent sure," I muttered. As we entered the building we met more kids from our school. They were also looking for information for their stories. The library wasn't too spectacular, but it contained many books about the local history. I checked the card boxes for titles. I found the aisle with the books I was interested in and stared at the numbers. A hand on my shoulder made me turn around.

"I found a great book for you, Rikst," Dirk stood right behind me. "Legends and folktales from Friesland. Sounds like what you might need," he said as he handed me the book.

"Oh," I mumbled. Feeling embarrassed, I didn't look

· 42 ·

up, knowing my face would be beet red. I didn't know what to say to Dirk. Was he serious or was he teasing me again?

"You're welcome," he chuckled and walked away.

My cheeks burned. I could have at least said thank you. His reaction was so different from the teasing I was used to.

"What's with him," Marijke pointed in Dirk's direction.

"I don't know, but I do need this book. Let's find what we need and get out of here. Already I'm starting to feel claustrophobic."

Marijke found two books about the castle in Buren and I found another with Dutch folktales. We hurried home. In the kitchen we each got a glass of milk and a piece of cake and headed upstairs to my room. We didn't talk much, as we both became engrossed in our research.

I started with the legends from Friesland. In the table of contents I found the legend of Rixt. Once I began reading I quickly forgot that Marijke was even in the room. I went back in time and learned about the woman whose name I bore. The story really captured me. I felt I walked with Rixt through the dunes. Listened with her to the sound of the rollers, thundering onto the shore. I followed her tracks in the sand and saw the treasures she gathered: barrels, crates, and colorful bottles.

Marijke finally broke the spell.

"I've taken so many notes, I'll have too much to write about. You lose marks when your story is too long," she said, while her pen kept scrawling.

"Did you find any interesting facts about your Rixt?" I asked.

Marijke nodded. "It's sad that the castle is gone. It would have made my story more interesting if I could actually visit and describe it. All I have to go by are the pictures in this book."

"But you're allowed to use your imagination. By looking at the pictures you can pretend you live in the castle and you'll be able to write about it."

"That's easy for you to say," Marijke added. "You can pretend anything and your imagination goes wild."

"Well, I must be kind of crazy," I grinned.

"Sometimes you are," Marijke smiled. "Now, tell me about your Rixt."

"Did you know she had a son named Sjoerd?"

Marijke shook her head. "All I know is that she lured the ships at night in stormy weather."

"And one morning after a storm she found a body on the beach. It was her long lost son, Sjoerd," I read.

"You have to admit, she's much more interesting than my Rixt," Marijke laughed. "Rixt van Doniah did a lot of boring things, like organizing charity meetings. But that was a pretty big thing because at the time many poor widows whose husbands had drowned in the sea lived on the island."

Then she changed the subject. "I'm finding it hard to concentrate on my writing, are you? All I want to think about right now is tomorrow's ball. And which costume Dirk will disguise himself in. Anyway," she sighed, a far away look in her eyes. "Have you made up your mind now? Will you write about Rixt from the bird sanctuary? You have to. You have so much information."

"I think I will. There isn't much time to research anything else. But please don't tell anybody."

Marijke's brown eyes sparkled. "You shouldn't let Dirk spoil it for you."

"Oh, Marijke, your face is all flushed. You have it bad, don't you?"

"Yes, I do like him. He's so handsome. But don't tell a soul. Linda and her gang will kill me. They all have a crush on him. You must admit, Rikst, he's the cutest guy in the whole entire school."

"You mean on the whole entire island," I snickered.

"Don't make fun of me, Rikst. That's not fair."

"Don't worry. I won't tell anybody your big secret. And you can have him. I hate Dirk. He's an arrogant horsehead. Now, let's change the subject and plan tomorrow night. Where shall we meet?"

"Let's meet here at quarter to five," Marijke answered. "Will you wear your costume?"

"No. It's kind of bulky. And I won't be able to get away fast enough if we get caught."

"I have the same problem. We can wear a dark curtain as a cape." She swung her arms elegantly around her as if pulling on a cloak.

"That's a great idea." I nodded. "But bring your costume here. We can have something to eat before we go to the dance."

After dinner I walked Marijke home and made her swear not to tell the class about my topic.

Later that evening I went back to my room to do more research. In another source I read that when Rixt found the bodies on the beach she cut off their limbs in order to collect jewelry. "Ugh." And I was named after her!

All the different versions of Rixt's legend gave me plenty to think about, but no clue about my name. I was fascinated by the legend and wrote down some of the most interesting details. How to start the story, I wasn't quite sure. Would a narrator tell the story, or maybe I could make up a friend who had known her? Hopefully it would come to me later. First I'd let all the information stew in my head. On the weekend I'd work on my first draft.

I went downstairs to try on my costume for a last fitting. Mom had done a great job. She's very creative, especially when designing costumes. The two heads looked weird. While I was admiring myself in the mirror, Mom came to stand behind me.

"It's hard to tell which head is yours and which is fake. Nobody will ever recognize you."

"Thanks, Mom." I made my voice dark and sinister. My claws groped around her waist. Bending my two heads I tried to kiss her. The kisses were a little off target. We danced through the dining room and Mom laughed. She had to stop and hold her stomach. My insides felt warm.

When Dad came home, we watched the news. To our surprise they showed pictures of the island with the latest update on the damage done by the recent storm. A reporter interviewed Piet, the lighthouse guard, who said what he felt should be done to prevent the lighthouse from being swept away during the next storm.

"Is something being done soon, Dad?" I asked.

"Yes. On Thursday the sand pump dredge will move into its place about two kilometers off the coast. If everything goes according to plan they'll start pumping the sand through the pipes by next Wednesday. The long pipes from the dredge to the shore will spew the sand onto the beach and the bulldozers can start moving the sand against the dune. The new dune will be planted with marram grass, which should keep the sand from blowing away again."

"Let's hope we don't get another storm before Monday," Mom said. She sat at the dining room table and opened a box.

"Jacob, the old beachcomber, came by today with a box full of things that he wants to donate to the museum. According to him the box contains valuables that he doesn't want his family to inherit when he dies. I didn't have time to go through all the stuff, but these little silver spoons caught my eye. I brought them home so that I could check my book on antique cutlery to find out where they came from and how old they might be."

I walked over to the table and picked up one of the spoons. The handle consisted of tiny little flowers forged from silver. Each small flower had five delicate petals.

"They are pretty, Mom."

"Yes, they are. And I know the perfect spot to display them."

"Did you find enough information for a story?" Mom asked, without looking up from her spoons.

"I don't know if it's what I want to write about," I replied. "Rixt must have been a horrible woman." I waited, hoping for some response.

But Mom remained immersed in her task.

"I'm going to bed. Good night."

.6.

"A surprise math test on the day of *Sunderklazen* ball?" Marijke's outraged voice shot through the classroom. All grade eight eyes turned to our desk and Marijke's face turned redder than a tomato.

"And Miss Marijke, what makes you think we cannot have a math test?" Mr. Visser peered over his reading glasses. A lock of greasy hair fell over his forehead. His long nose pointed at Marijke. "Do you need to put your costume on this early? You have another ten hours before the ball starts," his high voice screeched.

"It's a ... I'm sorry. I'm a little excited about tonight." She bowed her head.

My fist balled under the desk. Mr. Visser — alias Mr. Greaser — was the least admired teacher in the school. We were sure he hated kids. You never heard him coming. He wore these soft-soled shoes to sneak up on people. With his hair greased back, and his ancient, brown corduroy jacket, he seemed to live in a different time. He always did things to pester us, like giving this surprise math test on a day like today. Who could concentrate? Everyone's thoughts were on the ball and who would masquerade as the *Sunderklaas*. Last year it had been the principal. And the rule was that it could never be the same man twice.

"You think math is not important for girls?" Mr. Visser began ranting again. "You're right, Marijke." He

.48.

picked up a ruler and pointed it in her direction. "Girls don't have the brains for math. They don't get it. They'll never do well in math. But if you don't want to write this test; then, you know where you can go."

Now, I was ready to explode. Which age did he live in? I kicked Marijke.

Startled, she sat up straight. "I don't need to go to the principal's office, Mr. Visser, and I'm looking forward to writing the test."

"Well, well, listen to that." He put down the ruler and took a stack of papers from his desk. "You may hand these out, Marijke," he said in a sickly sweet voice.

Marijke left her desk, but not before she made a gagging face. Good for you, I thought. Many of the girls in this class were good in math. And I was sure Mr. Visser hated us for it.

The test wasn't all that hard. And Marijke probably did very well. Mr. Greaser would hold that against her, because she didn't fit his theory.

The rest of the day was wild. The noise level in the school must have been ten times higher than on normal days. Many students tried to trick others into revealing what they would wear. But most people didn't give in. During our last class Dirk snuck up behind me.

"I'll dance with every witch tonight, so I can't miss you," he laughed.

I just looked at him. The arrogant bastard. Did he really think that I would dress up as the witch from the bird sanctuary? I grinned so he wouldn't know how I really felt.

"Oh, you're looking forward to it. I can see it in your eyes, Rikst."

"And what will you be, Mr. Know-Everything?" I looked at him in disgust.

"You'll never find out." He disappeared around the corner but not before he'd shown me his attractive lopsided smile.

"What did he say this time?" Marijke caught up with me.

"He's going to dance with every witch tonight." I looked in her flushed face. "Oh, Marijke, you gave it away," I leaned against the wall. "Your face is beet red. I know what you're going to be."

"That's not fair," she pushed my arm. "You trapped me. And now I need to know your costume!"

"I'll show you when you come to my place after school. Do you have a curtain?"

"Yes," she kicked the wall. Pushing and laughing we went to geography, our last class! What we did in that class was a blur. The excitement for tonight had taken over my brains.

●●●

"If you pin a couple of safety pins in the top of the curtain, we can wear it as a hood." Marijke looked in my mom's sewing box. "Here." She held up a card with eight safety pins. "Perfect. Now we need a belt to hold the cape together."

I ran upstairs to find two belts. While we were readying ourselves to go out for *Sunderklazen,* Mom made dinner in the kitchen.

"I don't like the two of you roaming through the village." She sliced a piece of dark rye bread for us. "There are still crazy people out there who do beat up women and young girls when they're discovered."

"Don't worry, Mom. All the girls are out. And they won't get us. We'll be fast. That's why we aren't wearing our costumes yet."

Mom looked up from her task. "In those dark brown curtains you two look like monks," she smiled.

Upstairs in my parents' bedroom we admired ourselves in the mirror. Giggling and tripping over the curtains, we managed to get downstairs and then we were ready to go out.

"We'll start behind the houses," I whispered. The sides of my disguise were a little long, so I had to watch my step. Darkness had fallen and to add to the eeriness of this special evening, the moon had decided to stay hidden. For a moment I shivered in my cloak; then, the excitement took over and I felt my heartbeat quicken.

"Let's try to go to Main Street and catch up with the sweepers," Marijke whispered.

Adrenaline rushing through our bodies, we made our way through the back lanes, our eyes adjusting to the darkness, until we reached Main Street. Most street-lights had been turned off. The black shadows of the houses loomed up like dark ghosts. From the far end of town came the sound of sticks and horns. The banging echoed through the street, bouncing off the walls of the buildings on either side.

We stayed behind the hardware store and had a good view of the length of Main Street. We listened to the sound of running feet approaching. A group of boys came into view. They were dressed in the weirdest costumes; their white outfits contrasting with the dark shadows of houses and buildings. Swinging their sticks and blowing their horns, they moved closer.

"Check behind the buildings!" the leader shouted. The group dispersed in all directions, including ours.

"Go!" I pushed Marijke back. She stumbled over her cape, but held onto a gate.

"There! The outhouse!" I whispered.

As fast as we could, we ran from the store, climbed a fence and staggered across the backyard of an old summer cottage. The cloaks hampered us as we heard the sweepers come up from behind. In the darkness we found the door of the outhouse. Marijke opened the door. Something scuffled over our feet.

"A rat!" I screeched. We pushed each other inside.

An overwhelming stench enveloped us.

"Close the door!"

Marijke grabbed the door and locked it with the wooden bar.

"Oh, gross! Plug your nose!" I pinched my nose, but it didn't take long before my head felt it would explode; I needed air. We stood squashed against each other.

"I hope that rat was the only living creature in this stinking place," Marijke whispered. My body started shaking and I held onto my friend. Marijke giggled.

"Sh, the sweepers. They're close." I held my breath while we listened to running footsteps and tooting horns. Sticks banged on the walls of the outhouse. We held onto each other.

"Any women in here?" a voice called. The handle of the door rattled. It wouldn't take much to break the wooden bar that locked the door.

"No one can last long in a stinking outhouse," another voice said.

While we clung to each other, the banging went on for what seemed like forever. Sweat poured down my face. The stench invaded my sinuses. I visualized rats running over my feet.

As soon as the sounds of the sweepers moved on, I pushed open the door.

"Let's go home. I've had enough of this game," I said. "And I feel disgusting."

I pulled Marijke outside and we filled our lungs with the brisk freshness of the evening air. Stumbling over fences and the flapping fabric of the cloaks, we returned to our street. A car drove slowly towards us, the headlights illuminating us. I pulled the hood down over my face. A tingling sensation trickled down my spine. Grabbing Marijke's arm, I pulled her into the yard of one of the houses.

"What's the matter?" She struggled to free her arm.

"Sweepers," I said while I pushed her behind the house.

"They never travel by car. It's not allowed. How could you tell they were sweepers? The lights were so bright I couldn't see who was inside the car."

"I don't know. I just had a feeling they were sweepers. But you're right. They couldn't be." I felt safer behind the buildings. I wasn't going to tell Marijke that the car was a brown station wagon which had passed us at full speed a couple of days ago and that I had recognized the woman in the passenger seat. The woman with long, white hair. The strange tourist Piet, the lighthouse guard, had mentioned. The woman I'd seen standing on the dune?

Two trembling monks out of breath opened the kitchen door. Mom greeted us with a turned up nose.

"We know. We need a shower, Mom." I explained our adventure. Mom shook her head. We left our cloaks in the laundry room and dashed upstairs.

After a refreshing shower and more food, Marijke and I changed into our costumes. Marijke transformed herself into an unrecognizable witch; my troll costume blew her away. We spent ten minutes admiring each other in the large mirror in my parents' bedroom. In an attempt to dance with Marijke, we tripped and fell against Mom's dresser. We struggled to regain our balance, but when I let go of Marijke, my hand knocked Mom's music box to the floor. I gasped.

"Oh, no," Marijke whispered, "the swans are broken."

I swallowed and picked up the music box. The two ivory swans on the wooden lid had lost their heads. Marijke lifted them off the floor. In disbelief, we stared at the pieces.

"Your Mom will be upset," Marijke whispered. "I remember when we were little we were never allowed to touch the music box. Your Mom would open the lid and the two of us would sit on the bed and listen to the tune."

"We have this special glue Mom uses when she repairs stuff for the museum." I took the swan heads from Marijke. "Hopefully she can glue the heads back on."

I felt terrible. Mom was really attached to the music box. She often just held it in her hands and looked at the swans. At times like that she seemed to forget everything around her and go off to some faraway place.

We went back downstairs in a much more somber mood than when we went up. I placed the music box and the two swan heads on the kitchen table.

"I'm sorry, Mom. We didn't mean to break it. I accidentally knocked the music box off the dresser."

Mom stared at the table. For an instant I saw her eyes glistening. She looked up and in a fleeting moment I saw the loss in her eyes. I didn't understand. Her face grew blank. A faint smile covered up her emotions.

"I can fix it so no one will ever know," she said. I have this special glue that can hide the most painful scars." She placed the music box and the swan heads on the counter.

I didn't know what to say or what to think. I wished we'd never acted so silly in her bedroom. The hurt in my mother's eyes had shaken me.

Mom took her camera out of a drawer. "Are you ready? The two of you are unrecognizable."

Mom took pictures and at exactly eight o'clock, when the streets were free of sweepers, we headed out for the school.

"I'm glad your Mom took it so well," Marijke said.

"Yes," I agreed, but inside I felt a twinge of sadness, as if I had stepped on my mother's heart. I pushed the thought away and kept an eye out for the brown station wagon. Why did it drive through our street? I couldn't dwell on it any longer. We reached the school and I got caught up in the excitement.

The *Sinterklaas* committee had worked long hours

to decorate the gym with colorful streamers and balloons. Lamps had been covered with red and green crepe paper, creating a ghostly lighting. Traditional songs were played about Saint Nicholas' birthday. Students in the strangest outfits had filled the gym. Many hours of labor had gone into creating the costumes. Everyone took pride in not being recognized before the masquerade ended at midnight. At that hour the person dressed as *Sunderklaas* must reveal his identity. Marijke and I stayed close together and, when the music changed to more popular tunes, we danced, drawing attention from the others.

"We must look like a weird couple," I said.

Marijke had to help me drink my soft drink. She pushed the straw through the troll's mouth to find mine. We laughed so hard the inside of my head mask got all wet and sticky.

As the evening wore on, more and more strange creatures danced together in small and large groups. I tried to figure out where Dirk might be. He still hadn't kept his promise to dance with every witch in the room. Beside Marijke, there was only one other witch. At eleven o'clock the committee members started with games in one area of the gym. The other half of the room was for onlookers or people who decided they liked to dance to the music. Teams of two people, each with one leg in a burlap sack, had to race the length of the gym. Marijke and I decided to give it try. My vision was hindered by the big troll head and I couldn't run properly in the bulky costume. We ended up tangled together in a heap on the floor and never made it to the finish.

I had trouble getting back on my feet because I was a little off balance with my two heads. Then a rough looking Viking pulled me off the floor. I didn't recognize him as he led me over to the dance area, which wasn't lit well enough to observe details of his costume.

My mask, together with the green and red lighting, made it hard for me to see if his eyes were blue or brown. It was a great disguise. He was taller than I was, so it couldn't be Bas, even though some of the costumes were deceiving because of oversized heads. I still hadn't found Bas. The Viking danced with me for a while, but we didn't talk. I suspected it was Dirk, but if it were, I couldn't figure out why he would dance with a troll instead of a witch.

Finally the midnight hour gonged. A tall knight banged a drum twelve times. Everyone gathered around in a circle. At the sound of the last bong *Sunderklaas* stepped forward. All eyes turned to the man dressed in a white velvet gown trimmed with gold ribbon. Small gold stars decorated the front of the gown. Three large stars shone from a bucket-shaped hat, which covered a silver wig.

Rikst was unable to recognize his face. Besides a white beard and mustache, *Sunderklaas* wore large, gold-rimmed glasses. In his right hand he carried a long staff with bells on top.

Slowly *Sunderklaas* took off his hat. He ripped off his white beard and mustache. I couldn't believe my eyes. I grabbed Marijke's arm.

"It's Miss Oud!" I squealed. My hands instinctively started to applaud. As soon as other students discovered the real *Sunderklaas*, a loud booing mixed with cheers and applause filled the gym. This was against all the rules. A woman could *never* become a bishop. A man dressed in coveralls put a microphone in front of her. Her hair disheveled, Miss Oud took the microphone and asked for silence.

"I thought it was time for a change," she said in her calm voice. "We cannot continue the *Sunderklazen* tradition and ignore the changes in our society. We cannot let the men rule the streets anymore. For the next year we will reverse the tradition. On the next eve of the fourth of December, girls between the ages of twelve and seventeen will sweep the streets and the boys better watch out."

The applause was long and loud. I was glad the majority of the students agreed with the new rule.

A pirate who'd been standing beside me uncovered his face and said, "Equality, Rikst. Are you happy?"

"Bas, how did you know?" I finally pulled off my head, while Marijke unzipped my costume. I was glad to be free of the weight and the heat of the fur.

"I didn't recognize you," Bas laughed. "I recognized Marijke when the two of you were all tangled up on the floor."

Across the room, I watched the Viking take off his mask. Dirk's head appeared and he grinned at me. Quickly I turned away as I felt the heat creep up from my neck to my already burning face.

.7.

Thank goodness, classes started an hour later the next morning. But I still felt drowsy when the first bell rang. Everybody talked about last night's ball. Even the teachers said it was the best ball in years. Miss Oud had surprised everybody and she gained more popularity, especially from the girls.

Marijke and I went for a walk during lunch time, mainly to get fresh air and to stay awake for the rest of the afternoon. We took the path to the elementary school. We could hear excited screams from the playground. The students had caught the Saint Nicholas fever. Tonight everybody would receive gifts. We stopped when we heard the whinnying of a horse behind us. The bishop, dressed in his red velvet gown and mitre, rode his white horse. Walking beside him, holding the reins of the horse, was his helper Black Pete. We smiled and waved. "Welcome, Saint Nicholas."

"Well, hello, little girls. Did you behave yourselves this year?" Saint Nicholas pulled on the horse's reins.

"Yes, Saint Nicholas. We have been very good." Marijke giggled.

"Well, Pete. You should look in your sack and see if there's something in it for these little girls." The bishop pointed at his helper.

Pete let go of the reins and dropped the heavy burlap bag from his shoulder to the ground. He took a handful of gingernuts and handed them to Marijke. When he took two coloring books out of the sack, his big red smile went from ear to ear and his white teeth sparkled. "*Fol two little gills,*" he laughed and pinched my cheek. Pete's r's always sounded like l's.

"Thank you, Pete. Thank you, Saint Nicholas," we said in unison.

The bishop and his helper continued on their way to the school. We ran back giggling, in time for the first bell.

"Do you have time to come with me after school? Or do you still need to wrap presents for tonight?" Marijke asked. "My grandma gave me some money last night. I'd like to buy new jeans."

"No, I'm all ready. I even helped my dad wrap his present to Mom and I wrote a poem for it." I was pleased that I had found time on Wednesday to save Dad from embarrassment. "Lucky you. I wish I had some money to buy jeans. As always, I'm broke. But, I'll go with you."

At our lockers, we met Dirk. He stood tall and I must admit handsome, his backpack slung over his shoulder. Today he made no comments about dead bodies or witches, but he stared at me. Confused by his new behavior, I turned away. His dark, earnest eyes made me feel uncomfortable.

In silence, I followed Marijke out of the building. We still didn't talk when we picked up our bikes and set off to the store. I couldn't tell her about the experiences Bas and I had had on the beach. Marijke was my best friend, but she didn't share my love for the sea. She couldn't understand why I spent so much time on the beach. She hated storms and couldn't wait to go to school on the mainland next year.

We were close, but I often didn't tell her about the things Bas and I did together. We had decided not to tell anybody about the vanished corpse. It seemed as if we had a silent agreement that we wanted to find out more about the missing body, although I had no idea how.

When Marijke and I opened the door to the store, we realized many people had had the same idea we had. We had to push ourselves through the crowded aisles. The small room held enough jeans to clothe all the people on the island. Every brand name, style and size hung there. And if it wasn't in the store, the owner would get it from a garage behind the building.

Marijke knew exactly what kind of jeans she wanted to buy. Still it took a while before she could get an empty fitting room. While she changed, I looked at some of the jeans that I really liked. More people from my class walked into the store. When Marijke called me to check out her new jeans, I turned suddenly and bumped into a man who carried several pairs of pants over his arm. I banged my knee; he dropped all the pants.

"I'm sorry," I said.

"No, no, no. I am sorry!" he said in heavily accented English. As I helped him pick up the clothing, I realized how small he was, much smaller than I. He was also very thin, with short, black hair and small eyes. He wore a brown, leather jacket. A tourist from an Asian country, I thought. Thousands of tourists visited Ameland in the summer, but in the wintertime, they were few and far between. There was something I found odd about this guy. Didn't Piet from the lighthouse mention that one of the three tourists had been Asian?

"I've paid already. Thanks for telling me how nice they look on me," Marijke laughed. "What happened between you and that little guy?"

My face flushed. "We bumped into each other and he dropped all the pants he was carrying." I didn't mention the three strange tourists. We left the store, wished each other a good Saint Nicholas' Eve and exchanged gifts.

"Don't open it until you get home," Marijke said. "It's breakable."

"Thanks." I tucked the gift carefully into my backpack.

Friday nights were always fun. After Boukje arrived home on the ferry, Bas and his Mom came over for coffee, pop and chips. Boukje always had many interesting stories to tell about her life on the mainland.

On this night Bas and his mom would join us to celebrate Saint Nicholas' birthday. Our two families had celebrated the festivities together since Bas' father died. Thomas would be present as well. He'd shared Saint Nicholas' Eve with us for as long as I can remember.

After supper Mom moved the large laundry basket full of presents into the living room. Then we all went down to the pier to pick up my sister. Mom and Dad traveled by car. It was a moonless evening. Bas and I rode down on our bikes. The two light beams showed us the way.

The pier, stretching about one kilometer into the sea, was busy with cars and cyclists. In the distance we saw the lights of the ferry. It took forty-five minutes to an hour, depending on the tide, for the boat to cross from the mainland to the island. At the end of the pier we waited for the boat to moor.

"Rikst, look! There is the same car that passed us on the way from Hollum the other day." Bas pointed at a brown station wagon parked near my parents' car. A man was just getting out of the driver's side.

"That's the man I bumped into this afternoon," I whispered. I had already told him about the incident in the store. Bas only remembered Piet telling us that the three tourists, who had visited the lighthouse, had Scottish or Irish accents. I was sure he'd said one guy looked Asian.

In the meantime the boat arrived. The gangway was

hauled out and the passengers started to disembark. I searched for Boukje. The boat carried many students and many other people who worked on the mainland, all coming home for the weekend. Then I saw Boukje waving as she came down the gangway. I waved back and started walking towards the boat. The crowd was thick and people shoved and jostled to get to their family and friends. As I tried to make my way to Boukje, I suddenly found myself staring into a pair of cold, gray eyes. I shivered. Froze. My feet wouldn't move. Then the spell was broken and a woman in a black, fur coat and large fur hat pushed past me. I was left with a clear memory of those cold, gray eyes.

Two arms were flung around my neck.

"Hi, little sister. Did you get into any trouble this week?"

"Oh, yes. Lots of trouble." I tried to smile and shake off the feeling of apprehension. "But now that you're home, you can protect me from all the dangers of this island."

Dad took her luggage and Boukje settled into the car with Mom and Dad. Bas and I found our bikes. The brown station wagon had gone.

"I think I saw the woman again, Bas."

"Which woman? The woman with long, white hair?"

"Yes, I think so. I didn't see her cloak or her hair, but I saw her eyes. They were ice cold and looked right through me."

"Are you sure it was the same woman? I mean you never saw her up close."

"I know. I know, Bas. It WAS the same woman."

Later that night, I asked Boukje, "Did you see a woman in a fur coat on the ferry?"

"Yes, and the guy she was with was big and tall with red, curly hair. They spoke English with a funny accent."

Aha! Now the puzzle fell into place. The little Asian

guy waiting in the station wagon had picked up the woman and the big man. These were the three tourists who had visited the lighthouse and who had shown interest in the bunkers. All we needed to know was what happened to the body. For some unexplainable reason I felt these three had something to do with the body.

Thomas arrived as we came home from the ferry. Bas carried a box with gifts into the living room and placed it beside the laundry basket. We sat in a circle, while Mom and Boukje served hot chocolate.

"Rikst get the plate with almond spice cookies," Mom said.

As soon as everybody had their drink and cookies, the gift exchange began. Dad always created a whole ceremony. He handed everybody a gift, and then one at a time, we could unwrap it and read our poem. Bas received the first big gift. I knew it was one of Dad's jokes. After unwrapping several layers of paper, a note said he had to hand it over to his mom. Aunt Anna had to go through the same procedure until she had to pass the gift on to Boukje. By the time Boukje was finished unwrapping, the gift had shrunk to a jewelry box. Boukje was excited to find a delicate silver necklace with a Capricorn charm.

The evening went by quickly with much laughter and many good jokes. I received a note saying I had to search the workshop for my present, but when I got there a big sign read HA, HA. THE GIFT IS UPSTAIRS IN YOUR BED. When I finally retrieved the gift from under my covers, it contained warm flannelette pajamas with feet, and a poem about my cold feet.

Mom loved her new book about antique china. Aunt Anna received two tickets for an art show on the mainland, so Mom could accompany her. Dad got computer games which he said he wouldn't share for the first four weeks.

Everyone received a chocolate initial, a tradition Thomas had kept for many years. *Ocean Life*, a book about one of Thomas' interests, was greatly appreciated. It didn't take long for the old skipper to immerse himself in another world.

Bas opened his new book on woodcarving right away and started studying the various techniques. Boukje and I went upstairs and tried on our new jeans and sweatshirts. I added a delicate blue bottle to my collection — my gift from Marijke.

Exhausted, we finally went to bed. It had been an evening like all the other Saint Nicholas' Eves I can remember; fun-filled with laughter and jokes in the company of loved ones.

•••

The next day, Boukje and I went to the beach. My sister wanted to take pictures of the platforms just off the coast. She was working on a school project about the natural gas that was found in the North Sea. A bright, clear sky greeted us. We walked over the shell path with our winter jackets tightly closed at the neck. Wind rustled through the pine trees. We passed the hollow oak tree where, when we were little, we imagined little gnomes lived. I stuck my head inside the hollow and called, "Anybody home?" as we used to do.

"Sh," Boukje's gloved finger touched her lips, "They sleep during the day, remember." We giggled, crunching down the path. Two black crows flapped their wings and flew ahead of us. Boukje told me about school and the new friends she'd made. I told her about the storm and the vanished body.

"Oh, cripes. You mean a real body? I've never been able to figure out why you and Bas like beachcombing. You find the strangest things. It's just like Rixt from the bird sanctuary. She found a body one morning after a heavy storm. When she turned the body over it was her long lost son Sjoerd. That's all I remember from the legend."

"Yes, I know," I said. I thought about Rixt, too. A witch she may have been, but she was also a mother who had lost her son.

"Do you know why I was named after her instead of Grandmother Wietske?"

"No," my sister answered. "I always found it strange. I never asked. Did you?"

"Yes. Several times. Mom never answers me. She always talks around it."

"Why don't you ask Dad?"

We plodded through the sand to the sea and Boukje took her pictures.

It felt good walking along the shore. A sandpiper trotted ahead of us, its long fine beak pecking at shrimp and other small fish. I picked up some mussel shells. I breathed deep, long gulps of the salty-smelling air. My tongue tasted the salt on my lips. It felt as if this was the only air that could renew my energy. When my hood blew off, I let the cool wind play with the strands of my hair.

After lunch we visited our grandparents, Mom's parents. They lived on the east side of the town.

Grandpa had a large vegetable garden and Grandma Boukje loved baking cookies. Today she'd made seashell cookies filled with whipped cream.

"Those are my favorite, but I'm only allowed one," Grandpa smiled. "Too much cholesterol. I don't know why your Grandmother doesn't make them with something that doesn't contain cholesterol."

Grandmother had knitted Boukje a warm sweater with a Norse design in forest green and white. When Boukje tried it on, she looked like an ice princess, pretty and warm, ready to go skating. Grandmother looked proudly at her oldest granddaughter.

"Which colors would you like, Rikst? Now that Boukje's is finished, I don't want to get bored."

"Oh, I'd love one, Grandma," I said. "I'd like navy blue with a white design. Would you mind making it bigger than my size?"

"Oh you and your bulky clothes. What are you trying to hide?" Boukje poked me in my ribs.

"Nothing," I said. "You wear your clothes, I like to live in them."

I guess I want to hide my long limbs. My legs look shorter when I wear a long top.

Grandma laughed and shook her head. "I'll have you try it on before I sew the parts together," she said.

After supper Boukje went out with her friends. I went over to see Bas. Marijke had gone to visit relatives for the weekend.

Bas' house was built in the same design as ours. From the front door you entered a hallway with a large kitchen at the end. On one side of the hall was the living room; on the opposite side, the dining room. Aunt Anna, who painted watercolors, had turned the dining room into a studio. Upstairs were three medium-sized bedrooms and a bathroom. Downstairs, behind the kitchen, a door led to the shed and laundry room.

"I finished carving the sandpiper," Bas said. "Do you want to see it?"

I followed Bas into the shed. A workbench covered the long wall. On the table lay several pieces of driftwood and Bas' tools. The large piece he'd found after the storm on Monday lay in the corner.

"What will you make out of this piece?" I pointed at Bas' latest find.

"I don't know, yet. It's too big to make a bird. Maybe I'll try a person."

"What about a seal?" I suggested.

"I'll make something special." His brown eyes

gleamed as he looked the piece over.

"Here's the sandpiper." He handed the bird to me.

"Oh, Bas. That's incredible! It's exactly like the bird I saw this morning on the beach."

"It's a birthday present for your dad," he said. "He's very special to me. I hope you don't mind."

"No, of course not."

Bas' face had turned crimson. His body hunched forward. He moved away.

"I know he'll like this, Bas. He loves birds and animals. You're special to him too. You make up for the son he doesn't have," I said. Dad had actually never mentioned that he'd wanted a son, but he treated Bas like one of his own.

I studied the little sandpiper. Every detail was carved with such precision that the bird seemed to be alive, ready to peck food.

"Did you decide on your topic for the essay contest?" I asked.

"I went to the library, today. I'll write about Hidde Dirks Kat."

"I've never heard that name before."

"He hunted whales. In 1777, he made an unfortunate trip. He and his ship got lost between the icebergs and ended up in Greenland. Their boat was wrecked and they walked for several days until they found the Inuit people. Many crew members died. A year and a half later the survivors returned home."

"That sounds interesting," I said. "I have decided to write about Rixt. But don't tell anybody. Marijke knows, but she'll keep it quiet for a while. I don't want Dirk to find out. He was the one who suggested it."

"I won't tell," Bas said. "I'll proofread yours if you do mine. I'm a lousy speller."

"Did you pick up that video you were telling me about last night?" I asked.

"Yes, I did. Let's go inside to watch the movie."

•••

All day Sunday the stories of Rixt filled my head. That evening, when I finally sat down at my desk, ready to write the first draft, I felt excited. I stared at the white sheet in front of me. I could feel the story. Earlier in the day I had decided which approach to take. I didn't want to write about a witch; I wanted to make her more human. More human than the other storytellers portrayed her. In my mind I had tried to imagine what it would have been like to be an outcast. To be alone and try to raise a child. With no one to turn to. I had to give her a friend. I took up my pen and began to write...

A LIGHT IN THE DUNES
by Rikst de Bruin

"The witch is here. The witch from the bird sanctuary is here!"

The chant echoed in the streets as the woman walked along, her white hair flowing past her waist. Her ragged coat, blowing in the wind, hardly covered her swollen body. Her wooden shoes clip-clopped on the cobblestones. When Rixt approached, mothers dragged their children inside.

At the last house Rixt turned the corner and disappeared among the dunes. Tears streamed down her face as she was accompanied once more by loneliness. Thorns scratched her hands and legs as she followed the overgrown path to the end of the bird sanctuary.

There the little shack she had tried to fix with wood from daily beachcombing expeditions, had become her home. She felt relief that Aag, the village midwife and medicine woman, had agreed to help when her baby was due, which could be any day.

Lately the items she carried from the beach to her house weighed heavy in her arms. Often she had to stop to catch her breath. The heaviness of her body made it awkward to transport large planks or heavy boxes.

November storms roared frequently and the sea gave lavishly. Two weeks earlier she had found a large wooden box. It made a perfect crib. Along with the box, many bolts of colorful fabric floated in. Rixt made several trips to the beach that day to gather all the treasures and carry them over the dunes to her home. That night her limbs ached badly, and her back felt broken.

The next day she cleaned the box and lined it with some of the fabric. She made tiny clothes and diapers and even cut out a curtain for the only window in her cottage. Rixt stored away the rest of the fabric. She was almost prepared for the baby to be born. Her last responsibility was to walk the long way to the village, where she couldn't avoid the hostile looks from the faces behind their lace curtains. When she knocked on Aag's door, she had to forget her pride and ask for help.

Rixt had to admit she was scared to have the baby all by herself. During the five years she had worked on a farm, she had seen many calves being born. This was different. She was not a cow. This baby had changed her life. When the farmer's wife found out about Rixt's condition, she had been chased away like a stray dog. The farmer had been nowhere in sight when she had left the property that Wednesday afternoon in July.

For days she had slept in barns and had found enough food in vegetable gardens along the way. She didn't go home. She couldn't. Her mother had enough mouths to feed; that's why she had left five years ago. An uncle on her mother's side lived on the island. He had no family. Maybe she could keep house for him in exchange for room and board for her and the baby. But when she arrived on the island, Rixt was informed that her uncle had died the previous spring. He had left nothing behind. His house had been rented out to a young couple.

The uncle, a loner, had wanted nothing to do with the villagers. In return, the people had treated him as the village fool. When the islanders heard Rixt was related to this man, was pregnant, and had no husband, they treated her the same way.

Full of despair and lonely, Rixt often wandered in the dunes where the rabbits and the birds didn't treat her like an outcast. During one of these walks, she had stumbled upon the shack. At one time, people had lived there because next to the door was a well with a pump. This small cabin sheltered her during rainstorms and she decided to make it her home. Every day she went to the beach to gather treasures that floated in with the tide. She found bottles, furniture, pots and pans, cans with coffee, tea and other foods.

August gave her enough to eat. There were berries, leaves and wild roots. At night, she often wandered to the village to pick just a few vegetables from the gardens. Although she hated to kill animals, she experimented with snares to catch small game.

Rixt survived in this way until one morning at the end of November, when Aag found her lying on the cottage floor. The birthing pains were frequent and twisted her body. The young woman was in labor for many hours and it was not until dusk that she gave birth to a healthy son.

"And what shall we call him?" Aag looked at Rixt. She had washed the new mother and tucked her in.

"His name is Sjoerd. Sjoerd for Master," Rixt answered quietly.

"Master of what, Rixt? Master of the bird sanctuary?"

"Yes, master of the bird sanctuary." A smile lit her face as she closed her eyes.

Aag shook her head, closed the door and walked back through the dunes to the village. She had delivered many children in the last forty years, but never a master of the bird sanctuary.

Sjoerd grew up to be a healthy toddler. As soon as his little feet could hold him, he trotted behind Rixt through the dunes to the beach and helped carry items from the sea back to their house. He learned the names of all the wild flowers, the birds *and the animals. He helped his mother in the herb and vegetable garden. Rixt never sent her son to school.*

•••

I stopped writing. My right hand hurt. I flexed it. When I rubbed it with my other hand, slowly the cramped feeling left. Turning to the beginning of my story, I read what I'd written so far. It probably needed to be cut, I thought. It was getting a bit long. I'd worry about that later. This was only my first draft.

After a stretch, I continued Rixt's tale...

•••

During these years the only visitor to the cottage was Aag. She came once a week to get herbs for her remedies. In return, she brought milk, eggs and flour.

When Sjoerd grew older, he often watched the big ships passing by in the distance. One day Rixt took him to the harbor where he could watch the fishing boats and the ferry. From that day Sjoerd often wandered to the harbor by himself. Rixt watched him go. He stood tall with broad shoulders, white-blond hair like his mother, and round, red cheeks. He didn't need to tell her where he was going. Even so, she felt a tightness in her chest, an unexplained fear.

On his eighteenth birthday Sjoerd announced, "I want to hire on in the spring. I'll go to the mainland and find a ship to work on in one of the seaports."

"You can't leave me alone, Sjoerd. I've always looked after you," Rixt pleaded. The thought of her son leaving her almost choked her.

"I'm grown-up, Mother. I can take care of myself."

In the months to come Rixt begged her son to stay with her. But when spring arrived, he left. With heaviness in her heart, Rixt waved good-bye.

"Mother, I'll be back with enough money to build you a real house with everything in it, so you don't need to roam the

beaches in stormy weather."

Except for Aag's visits Rixt had no contact with other people. But even those visits became less frequent for Aag's arthritis made it difficult for her to walk through the dunes.

Loneliness and longing did strange things to Rixt. Her wanderings along the beach became longer and more frequent. Not even the worst storm kept Rixt away. More and more treasures were dragged across the dunes to the old cottage. She wanted everything the sea had to give.

One day in the summer a man leading a cow came down the path to Rixt's cottage. It was Piet Dykstra, the old skipper. It was said that he was not afraid of anything, not even the devil.

Rixt met him on the path.

"The cow is yours, Rixt. Aag died last week and she wanted you to have the animal. Her name is Mintsje. She doesn't give a lot of milk, but enough to get you through the winter."

Rixt stared at the cow. The cow stared at Rixt. Long after Piet had headed back to the village, she realized she couldn't just stand there holding the lead to the cow. A fence had to be built. The cow needed food.

As time passed, Rixt grew fond of the cow. She told Mintsje all about Sjoerd.

"He is a handsome young man and a good sailor. When Sjoerd comes back, Mintsje, you have to give more milk. Half a pail is not enough for two healthy people."

That next fall the weather stayed calm, and the sea didn't give her the goods she needed. Day after day Rixt returned from her walks with nothing but a few pieces of wood.

"We need storms, Mintsje," she complained. "You have to help me."

Finally one night in November a storm blew up. Rixt tied a rope around Mintsje's neck. Taking a storm lamp and matches with her, Rixt led the cow through the dunes. Even though the night was moonless, she found her way. They moved slowly. Mintsje often stumbled into holes and over grass clumps. She led the cow to the top of the highest dune. There, she lit the lamp and tied it onto the rope under Mintsje's chin. Rixt stared into the dark. Yes, there were boats on the North Sea tonight. They stayed for hours on top of the dune, the woman and the cow.

Next morning before dawn Rixt walked down the dunes on her way to the beach. She almost ran along the shoreline. Wooden crates, large and small tins and other debris were spread out all over the sand. She watched the tide come in. Each wave brought in more items from a stranded ship. With the light of day, clouds moved in. Rixt gathered and piled wood, clothes, food and other items from the wreckage. She worked hard all morning. Then she remembered that Mintsje needed to be milked. She hurried one last time along the shoreline.

Then she saw it. A shape in the sand. Was it a body? Rixt shivered with the thought. The wind howled. Black clouds opened and sent down their rain. Rixt walked slowly. She kept her eyes on the bulk in the sand. Her heart pounded wildly.

She stopped a few steps away. Oh, my God! It was a body! Her mind screamed! Rixt stared at it. She looked around the dunes. Along the beach. Not one soul was out there. She was alone with the body. A man's body? He lay face down in the sand. His brown clothes were plastered with sand. He'd lost one boot.

Slowly, Rixt knelt down. She placed one hand on his shoulder and one on his hip, and turned him over.

Carefully she wiped the sand from his face and hair. The hair was white-blond. With horror in her eyes, she stared into the face.

"SJOEOEOEOERRRRD!!!" The storm carried her scream over the dunes and into the village.

Rixt carried her son home where she buried him amongst her herbs. Rosemary, thyme and lavender covered his body.

After the tragic loss of her son, Rixt found no rest. For days and nights she wandered through the dunes and along the beach always calling his name. One day Piet, the skipper found *her lying in the sand. A blanket of long white hair covered her shrunken body. Her ragged clothes were plastered with sand. He looked at her face, in death it looked somehow younger than it had when she was alive. As if she had finally found peace.*

The old skipper carried her home and buried her beside her son in the herb garden, the place she had tended with love for so many years.

To this day the people on the island can tell you about the ghost of Rixt, who wanders over the bird sanctuary. Many people have seen her — a lonely figure walking along the beach, her long, white hair blowing in the wind. At night, when storms rage across the island, one can hear her screams all the way to the village, "SJOEOEOEOERRRRD!! SJOEOEOEOERRRRD!!"

•••

Eleven o'clock. Letting out a long sigh, I put down my pen, rubbed my neck and my sore hand. I read the story over once more, then, put it in my drawer. I went downstairs to get a drink and say good-night to my parents. Tired, but satisfied, I crawled under the covers and turned off the light. Tomorrow I would read the story over and fix it up. Then, Bas could check it for me.

A loud noise woke me. "Ouch!" My hand hurt.

I sat up and felt confused. After a few seconds I realized I must have had a nightmare. I'd hit my alarm clock. The loud noise was the clock hitting the floor. I picked it up. Three o'clock. My dream, what was it about? Slowly, the images came back to me.

I stood on top of a dune waving a light back and forth. I wore a long, white gown. My hair blew in the wind. The lights of many ships all came in my direction. I had wanted to warn them that the harbor was on the other end of the island. I had waved my arms and hit the alarm clock.

.8.

Caught up in family activities, Bas and I didn't go back to the beach or visit Thomas on the weekend, although I was dying to know if there had been any news about the body. The *Amelander News* didn't mention it. Perhaps the police had decided to keep it secret or had concluded that it was not worthwhile to investigate the matter further.

Sunday night Dad and I drove Boukje to the ferry. When we arrived, I was surprised to see the brown station wagon in the parking lot. As Boukje purchased her ticket I noticed the big Irishman, the woman with the long, white hair and the Asian standing side-by-side on the top deck of the ferry.

"Keep an eye on the woman with the white hair and the cold eyes. Let me know if she acts suspiciously," I whispered to my sister when it was time to say good-bye.

"Oh, you're imagining things, little sis," she smiled. "You should become a detective when you grow up. But I'll fill you in on any dubious behavior when I call home Wednesday night."

Later that night I went over to visit Bas and told him that our three 'tourists' had left the island.

"Strange," Bas said. "They just came back Friday night."

I nodded.

Later that evening during supper I brought up the subject of my name, but Mom ignored the whole question and talked about this history course she had signed up for on the mainland.

I decided that Boukje's suggestion about asking Dad would probably be a good idea. He was always pretty straightforward. It was worth a try.

The opportunity to talk to my father alone didn't occur until Monday, when Bas and I went over to the western part of the island after school to watch the preparations for the work on the dune. We saw the sand pump dredge way out in the sea. The large pipe was lying on the beach, ready to spew sand. Dad was supervising the project.

"Hi, Dad!" I waved as I saw him walking towards us.

"Hi, Uncle Jan!" Bas shouted.

"Put your bikes down and come over. I want to show you what we've done!" he called.

We parked our bikes at the lighthouse gate and ran down the dune to where Dad stood.

"The pipe is almost in place," he said. They have to attach the ends of the pieces of pipe together. Watch the men on the small boat. They'll assemble the next length before they lift it overboard."

We watched the work in progress.

"The bulldozers will arrive tomorrow," Dad said. "By Wednesday I expect them to be ready to pump the sand onto the beach. Then the bulldozers will push the sand up against the dune. After that job is done they'll plant the marram grass."

I tugged at his coat. Dad turned his head.

"Can I talk to you, or do you have to stay here?"

"Sure," he said. "Let's go for a walk."

I told Bas that we wouldn't be long and followed my dad to the shoreline.

"What is it you want to talk about?"

Dad always made it easy. He wasn't like Mom. You had to spell it out for her. Dad was more sensitive in those matters.

"I'd like to know what the big secret is about my name," I started.

"The big secret about your name?" Dad repeated, a frown creasing his forehead.

"Yes, every time I ask Mom why I was named after the witch of the bird sanctuary, she avoids the answer. She ignores the whole question and starts talking about something else. How come I wasn't named after my grandmother like Boukje?"

Dad looked at me. His eyes shone deep blue. They always got darker when he became serious or when he was deep in thought.

"Rikst, I know this is difficult for you to understand." He looked away. "Mom will tell you, but you have to give her some time. It is not easy for her, but she will tell you. She just isn't ready yet."

"I don't understand, Dad. What can be so difficult about it? And why can't you tell me if she isn't ready?"

Dad stared over the sea. I was confused. Angry. I hadn't expected that kind of answer from Dad. I had expected a straight answer from him and now he was beating around the bush just like Mom.

"It's not fair!" I said, tears filling my eyes. I kicked the sand with my boots. It sprayed in front of us and splattered our pants. I took a deep breath. It was no use getting angry. I would only make it worse.

Dad stopped and faced me. He grabbed my hand.

"Let's go back. And Rikst? Promise me you'll be patient with Mom? She will tell you in time. I can't. Mom has to do it and I know she will. Just don't pressure her."

We walked back in silence. Bas still watched the sand pump dredge and the men working on the small boat.

I didn't want to stay any longer. My mind was on a merry-go-round. Why was it so difficult for Mom to tell me? Why did she have to be ready? What secret was she hiding?

Bas sensed my mood.

"You want to take the back roads or the main road?" he asked.

"Let's take the back roads. It's quieter."

We took our bikes and waved at the lighthouse guard. Two rabbits hopped across the path into a blackberry bush. We pedaled past the bunkers, but today I didn't really look at the signs on the barbed wire fencing until Bas stopped suddenly, his tires skidding in the sand. I put on the brakes and stopped beside him.

"What's wrong?" I asked.

"See these tire tracks?"

"What about them?" I asked.

"They are leading into the bush."

I watched his hand point at a rosehip bush. A set of car tracks went around the bush and into a clearing.

"Why would someone take the car off the road here?" Bas said. "You could easily get stuck here in the sand."

"Let's follow the tracks." I'd forgotten about the conversation on the beach with my dad. I smelled adventure.

Bas looked at me. A flicker of doubt crossed his eyes.

"Come on, Bas. What are you waiting for? Or aren't you game today?" I challenged.

"Of course," he said. "Let's hide our bikes under these bushes.

We pushed them both under the branches and covered them as much as we could.

"Why hide them?" I asked. "You make it real spooky."

Bas laughed. "You never know."

I followed Bas up the dune in the tracks. It must have been a four-wheel drive. A normal car wouldn't get far in this sand. In the middle of the slope the tracks made a left turn.

"It's leading to the bunkers," I said.

Bas nodded. "You're right."

Our bodies bent low to stay out of sight, we walked to the top of the dune. Once we got near the top of the rise, Bas signaled for me to stop. Carefully he raised himself up until he could see over the top of the dune. And immediately he threw himself down, almost knocking me off my feet.

"What did you see?" I panted.

"There's someone at the bunker."

"You mean inside the barbed wire fence?" I asked.

"Yes! Stay low. We don't want be seen."

Slowly I raised myself onto my knees. I made sure most of my head stayed hidden in the marram grass. The tough blades scratched my face. Cautiously I looked in the direction of the bunkers.

"I don't see anybody now." Bas moved up beside me.

"Let's wait."

The minutes passed as we stared at the bunkers. We didn't see any movement. Then the sound of a car engine, from the direction we'd come, startled us.

"The car!" Bas panicked.

"Quick!" I said. "Let's go over the top. We can hide in those bushes at the bottom."

The sound of the engine died away and we heard a car door slam. We threw ourselves over the top of the dune and rolled down and into a clump of hawthorn bushes. A great hiding place! The thorns scratched our hands and faces. When Bas pulled me down at the bottom of the dune, the sleeve of my jacket ripped.

Out of breath, we lay as still as possible. I moved my head so I could see the dune.

"I'm so glad we hid our bikes," I whispered.

Bas nodded. "Look," he said, his head pointing at

the top of the dune.

I held my breath. There, on top, stood the woman with the long, white hair and the little man I had bumped into in the jeans store.

"They are back from the mainland. It's Ice-woman and the little Asian guy," I whispered.

"Why'd you call her Ice-woman?"

"Because of her cold, gray eyes and her long, white hair."

"They're heading for the bunker." I followed Bas' gaze.

"Look, there's a hole in the barbed wire fence," Bas pointed.

We watched the two climb inside the wire. They disappeared around the bunker.

"What do we do now?" I whispered. "Wait, or get out of here?"

"If we leave, we have to do it fast." Bas looked at me.

"Let's go." I got up onto my knees, but Bas pushed me down.

"There's someone outside the bunker. It's the big, Irish guy. He's wearing binoculars. Head down! He's looking in this direction."

My heart started beating wildly in my chest. "What would they do if they found us spying on them?" I whispered.

"You better not try to imagine," Bas answered.

Though we were well hidden, the memory of the cold, gray eyes of the Ice-woman stopped my breathing. We stayed low until the man finally turned away and went back behind the bunker.

"Now crawl!" Bas pushed me.

I tried to inch my way up on my stomach. Panting and groaning, I pushed myself forward on my elbows until we finally reached the top. I looked behind me, but didn't see anybody at the bunker. As if on a signal, we rolled down the other side of the dune. Sand and twigs flew into my face and my mouth. There was no sign of a car or truck, though there were more tracks in the sand.

"They took the car around into the clearing, hidden from the road." Bas quickly recovered our bikes and without brushing our clothes off, we jumped on them. Out of breath, we pedaled for our lives.

We hadn't ridden far when a car sped up behind us and sounded its horn. *Beep!* Startled, Bas and I pulled our bikes over close to the shoulder of the road. Bas moved behind me. A brown station wagon covered with sand raced past.

"That's them!" I shouted over my shoulder.

Then, a short distance ahead of us, the car braked dramatically. It didn't quite come to a complete stop, but seemed to be waiting for us to catch up. There was nothing we could do but keep pedaling. As we approached I could see that it contained the three people we'd seen at the bunkers. The big Irishman drove, Ice-woman sat in the passenger seat and in the back sat the Asian guy.

"Don't slow down," Bas coached from behind me. "Just keep going!"

Now I was really scared! These people were definitely not your normal tourists. They acted too suspiciously. Something told me that they suspected us. What were they going to do now? Had they seen us on the dunes? How could we get away from them out here on this back road?

The car was barely moving now and we could not avoid coming up alongside it. Ice-woman rolled down the window.

"Excuse me," she said in a heavy, Irish accent. "Can you tell me where we can rent bicycles?"

"In … in the next v-village," I stammered, as I tried to keep pedaling at a steady pace. "Ask for No- Nobel

Bicycle rentals." My proficiency in English wasn't that great, but in spite of my anxiety, I'd pulled it off.

All three seemed to be staring intently at Bas and me. Once again I felt the force of Ice-woman's gaze. She seemed to look right through me. I felt she was trying to stare me down, but I was able to look away in order to keep my bike on the road.

"Thank you," she said finally. She rolled up the window and the car sped away.

Once the station wagon had disappeared from sight, I stopped riding. I dismounted, dropped my bike on the ground and flopped down beside it. I thought my heart would explode in my chest. My face felt hot and flushed. My hands trembled.

Bas plunked down beside me.

"They already knew where to rent bikes. There are signs all over town," he snorted. "Did you notice how they looked us over?"

"Yes," I answered. "That was just an excuse to get a close look at us. But we also got a good look of them. Did you see the big, red scar the driver had on the right side of his face? It went from his ear almost to his chin."

"What do we do now?" Bas got up on his feet and retrieved his bicycle.

"We should tell Thomas and the police," I followed Bas. We bicycled in silence until we reached the edge of town.

"First, let's go home," Bas announced. "After supper we'll visit Thomas."

"But I'm not allowed," I answered. "My mom won't let me bike to the bird sanctuary after dark."

"Let's do it tomorrow after school then," Bas said. "I better get my story ready for you to proofread."

•••

Later that evening I went over to Bas' house.

"Here is my short story for you to read. I'm nervous and not sure if I want to hand it in the way I wrote it. Your opinion is important to me. Tell me if I made Rixt too nice? The story is also too long."

"Don't worry, I'll chop it for you. And here's mine." He handed me his copy which was neatly typed. "It looks good until you check the spelling," he chuckled.

Back in my room I read Bas' story and spent a long time fixing it up. The story interested me and I learned more about the people on the island than when I read the history books.

Once I had finished working on Bas' story, I remained sitting at my desk. I tried to come to terms with the business of Rixt and my name. Since I'd written the story a sadness, which I found hard to describe, had come over me. By identifying with her, I had become aware of what it must have been like to live as a castaway. What loneliness and hardship she must have endured! No wonder she went crazy in the end.

And then I realized I didn't really want to change my name. But I still couldn't understand the secrecy surrounding why I was named after her. My mother must have a good reason. Why wouldn't she tell me?

.9.

"But what could they be doing in the bunker?" I watched Thomas' expression. We sat around the kitchen table in his cozy cottage.

Thomas puffed on his pipe. Ringlets of blue smoke circled his face. "They could use the bunker to hide things," he said in a deep voice.

"Like a body," I added.

Thomas nodded. "If indeed they were the ones who took the body."

"You do believe we saw the body, Thomas?" Bas said. "We didn't make it up."

"I do believe you. I also believe that Rikst saw the ghost of Rixt."

"I don't think it was Rixt's ghost. I think it was Ice-woman," I said.

"That's possible, too," Thomas nodded. "What do the two of you intend to do with this information?"

"We have to go to the police," Bas answered. "But I feel pretty stupid telling them about our suspicions without any evidence. The only thing that the police might find interesting is that the three of them trespassed inside the barbed wire fence of the bunker. Even though that's hard to prove." Bas sighed.

"Perhaps we should gather some more information before we visit Officer Kiewiet," Thomas got up from his chair and took a piece of paper out of the top drawer of the kitchen cabinet. "This is what we have so far," he said. "A brown station wagon, three people, a woman with long, white hair, a man with red, curly hair and a scar on the right side of his face." He wrote the information down.

"The man is tall and big," I added.

"Then, there's the short, skinny man of Asian appearance," Thomas looked up from his notes. "They are interested in the second bunker, the one that's hidden from view of the lighthouse. We also have a body that's lost. Good." Thomas put down his pen.

"And Friday night the big Irishman and Ice-woman came on the ferry from the mainland and Sunday night the three of them left," I added. "Today all three of them were back on the island. And Thursday night the station wagon drove very slowly down our street." Bas' eyes widened. "Sorry, I forgot to mention it before."

"Did they see you?" Bas voice sounded concerned.

"Marijke and I were disguised as monks, so I don't think they recognized us."

"Right." Thomas took notes as I spoke. "The first thing we have to find out is where they're staying. Tomorrow morning I'll do a little tour on the island. I'll even ask some people in the stores and perhaps I'll pedal over to Nobel's Bicycle rentals in Buren."

"What can we do?" I asked. Now my adrenaline was flowing. I loved it. The excitement mingled with apprehension. I had no idea what we'd get ourselves into. "We have to take into consideration that these people could be dangerous," Thomas added. "They might carry weapons. Tomorrow after school, you two go back to the west end, to check out the repair work on the dunes. Leave your bikes at the lighthouse and approach the bunkers through the dunes. That way you run less chance of being seen from the road. Find out if there are any activities going on at the bunkers. Tomorrow night we'll meet back here."

"We might have more information to take to the police," Bas said.

"I'm not allowed out to go bicycling after supper," I said.

"I'll talk to your mom about that at the museum tomorrow," Thomas said.

"Okay, I don't know if that will work, but it's worth a try," I smiled. Knowing my mom, she wouldn't give in. Not even to Thomas.

"We'd better go," Bas said. "I still have to rewrite my whole story," he winked at me.

"Try to remember how to spell simple words like 'shipwrecked,' with a 'ck,'" I teased. "Thanks, Thomas. We'll see you tomorrow after you've battled with my mom."

When we left the skipper's cottage, it was already getting dark. On overcast days like today the sky darkened at five o'clock.

"I finished reading your story, Rikst," Bas said as soon as we turned onto Sand Dike.

"What'd you think of it? Did I make her too nice?"

"You did show a different Rixt than the one in the legends I've read, but what I liked about your story is that you made her human. No one has ever looked at her as a person with feelings, fears and anxiety. Nobody thought of her as a mother. That's what came across in your version. It is a sad story. I only made suggestions. It is a bit lengthy and you know they take marks off."

"Thanks, I appreciate your opinion."

"And I appreciate you correcting my spelling. I cannot afford to lose too many marks in my Dutch class."

Just before we turned into our street, I stopped. "Wait, Bas. Do you see that car parked past your house?"

"It's the station wagon!" Bas turned his bike around. "We'll go in the back way. Follow me."

As we struggled with our bicycles through backyards and over fences, I wondered if our three 'tourists' had found out where we lived. It couldn't be possible. Had they seen us at the bunker? Were they following us as we were following them?

"We better keep an eye out for these people," Bas warned when I turned into our property.

Mom was busy at the stove cooking pasta, my favorite.

"Mmm, that sauce smells good, Mom," I said as I plopped down at the kitchen table.

"Homemade," Mom stirred a pot with boiling tomatoes, peppers, onions and who knows what. Mom seemed a little tense. The sharp lines edged around her mouth meant frustration or tension. I wondered if Dad had told her about our conversation the other day on the beach.

"I had some strange visitors at the museum today." Mom interrupted my thoughts.

I looked up, "What kind of visitors?"

"Remember the three people you talked about?"

"Yes."

"I'm sure it was them."

I held my feet still on the kitchen floor. It probably was, I thought. And those strange people were now spying on our houses. But I didn't mention it. Mom would want to call the police and mess things up for us.

"They probably were from Ireland, because they spoke with that kind of accent, except for the one man. He looked Asian and hardly spoke."

I held my breath. "Did the woman have long, white hair and did the Irishman have a scar on his face?"

Mom nodded.

"They wanted to know what kind of articles could be found on the beach and if there were still beach-combers around these days. They also asked me about Rixt."

"Rixt?" I gasped.

"Yes," Mom continued. She removed the saucepan from the stove and filled a pot with water for the spaghetti. "Most foreigners don't know about the legend. That's what really surprised me."

"What did you tell them about her?" My fingertips tapped on the table.

"Just the general legend, how she roamed the beaches and lured the ships and that one day she found a body and it was her long lost son."

"Oh," I said. "Did you have the feeling that she knew the legend?"

"Why?" Mom looked at me surprised.

"I just wondered. Why would a foreigner from Ireland want to know about Rixt, if she already acted like her?"

"Perhaps she's seen the statue and became interested." Mom stirred spaghetti into the boiling water. "She did have the strangest eyes. Gray and cold. When she looked at me, she made me feel very uncomfortable. I felt threatened by those eyes."

"That woman was on the ferry last Friday and again on Sunday night. And I saw her in town. I think it's also the same woman I saw on top of the dune the day Bas and I found the body on the beach. I call her Ice-woman."

"The name suits her. Rikst, will you set the table? Dinner is ready and I hear Dad's car in the driveway."

"So, how are the short stories?" Dad asked while the three of us enjoyed our meal.

"Can I read yours before you hand it in?"

"Yes, but I still have to rewrite it." I hadn't thought of letting anybody beside Bas read my story. "Bas said I needed to make a lot of changes."

"I don't mind typing it for you on the computer," Mom said. "Thursday is my day off."

"I'll see. Thanks, Mom. Could Bas and I visit Thomas after supper tomorrow? He wants to know how the repairs on the dunes are going, and he will give us some ideas for the short story contest," I lied.

"Can he not go there to see for himself?" Mom asked with concern in her voice.

"I don't know," I mumbled. My face grew all hot. I hated lying and I wasn't very good at it. But if I told my parents that we were investigating the behavior of those three strange tourists, I wouldn't have any chance of being allowed to go.

"I thought you'd finished your story," Mom added.

"What time would you be back?" Dad asked.

"Around eight or eight-thirty," I was surprised Dad got involved. He usually lets Mom deal with curfew and the other rules of the house.

Mom looked at Dad. Dad nodded.

"No later than eight-thirty then," Mom said. Her face told me she didn't agree.

"Okay, thanks, Mom. And Thomas is coming by the museum tomorrow to ask if it is all right."

Mom sighed.

Tuesday nights it's my turn to wash the supper dishes. Afterwards I went upstairs to rewrite my story and to study for my history test on Thursday. I figured I might not have enough time tomorrow night and there was a lot to study. The test was about the French Revolution and the time of Napoleon.

Wow, Bas had done some major cutting, I thought as I read my story. I didn't agree with everything he wanted me to leave out, but I did follow most of his suggestions. After I'd finished I thought about Mom's proposal. If she typed the story for me, she would read it, too. I wasn't sure yet if I wanted her to read it. But if I went out tomorrow night, I might not have time to type it myself.

First, I had to concentrate on my history. Tomorrow after school I would go back to the west end of the island and find out what our three tourists were up to. Excitement and fear filled my thoughts when I remembered how Bas and I had crawled over the dune and watched them. Mom hadn't been pleased with the rip in my jacket. Again I had lied, claiming I'd fallen off my bike.

.10.

"Look at the heap of sand. Hopefully that will keep the dunes in place when the next storm roars in from the northwest." I watched the sand being spewed onto the beach from the dredge pipe. Four bulldozers plowed the sand against the dune. The noise of the bulldozers was deafening. Flocks of seagulls hovered above the sand spout.

I didn't see Dad. We parked our bicycles at the lighthouse and took the northern trail to the conservation area.

We left the path and cut through the dunes to the bunkers. A pheasant flew out of its hiding place and startled us both. The long colorful tail feathers indicated it was the male of the species.

"Stay as low as possible," Bas suggested.

This time we went around the first bunker and found a hiding place between the barbed wire fence and the bushes at the back of the shelter. I found it amazing how well the bunkers were hidden. Covered with sand, marram grass, plants and bushes, the bunkers were completely concealed, except for the entrances. You had to know where to find them.

"We have a good view of the back door of the second bunker," I whispered, while I tried to get as comfortable as possible.

"It might be a long wait," Bas shifted on his knees

until he settled into a position where he could scan the side of the bunker as well.

"We'll probably have to wait until dusk," I sighed.

Bas nodded. His eyes stayed focused on the shelter in front of us.

"Brrr. It's cold here." I felt the cold of the sand penetrating my jeans.

"We have to find more evidence. That's why we're here," Bas reminded me. "Listen. That sounds like the engine of a car."

I focused on the sound. The light now had faded and dusk was settling in. The shadows of bushes all merged into creature-like shapes.

"There! A flashlight," I pointed in the direction of the bunker.

The beam of a small light came around the bunker. I grabbed Bas' sleeve. Now we had a chance to find out more about what these strangers were doing in the bunker.

"Watch," Bas pointed. "That's the big Irishman. He's carrying a box."

The man opened the back door.

"They must have a key," I whispered.

"I wish we could move closer," Bas suggested. "There's Ice-woman. She's also carrying a box. I wonder what they're taking into the bunker? Where's the Asian guy?"

"I hope he's not guarding the area," I shivered. I didn't want to be found. Some gut feeling told me we shouldn't underestimate these people.

"There he is," Bas pointed. "Now that they're all inside, let's try to get closer to the second bunker."

I wasn't sure if I agreed with his idea, but I followed Bas slowly on my hands and knees.

"Are you sure they won't see us when they come back out?" I whispered.

After we'd settled behind a very prickly bush, I had to admit we had a good view of the back entrance, but we were also awfully close to the bunker. I was convinced that if they shone a flashlight into the bushes they would be able to see us clearly.

"Sh," Bas put his hand on my arm.

The door opened and Ice-woman walked out. She carried a flashlight and shone it in the direction of the first bunker. I held my breath. She walked over to the other shelter and seemed to aim the light directly at the bushes we had previously occupied. Bas gripped my arm. We watched as she slowly returned to the second bunker, the beam of the flashlight making wide arcs in front of her. The door to the bunker opened and the Irishman joined her outside. Ice-woman pointed the flashlight around the other side of the bunker. Before they crawled through the opening in the barbed wire fence, the big man turned around. It was as if he stared right at us. Perspiration trickled down my spine. My heart pounded so hard, I was sure he could hear it. Now he would discover us! But he seemed to change his mind because, after a brief hesitation, he crouched down and followed Ice-woman through the fence.

"The Asian guy is still inside. What do we do now?" I shivered.

"Let's wait a little longer," Bas answered.

"I need to go home, Bas. If I'm late for supper, my mom won't let me go to Thomas' tonight."

"All right. Let's go."

"We should go back to the first bunker and leave the way we came," I suggested.

Bas nodded. We crept back to the bushes of the first shelter. Once out of sight, we returned through the dunes to the lighthouse. We pedaled home in silence, each of us occupied by our thoughts.

So we now knew that they used the bunker for a

hiding place. But what was in the boxes they'd carried inside? Weapons, explosives, alcohol, drugs? A couple of years ago, the police had caught a gang who smuggled cheap alcohol into Norway using fishing boats.

Thomas would have found out more information by now. We definitely had to go to the police.

After supper we hurried to Thomas' cottage. It was such a clear night, with a full moon and millions of stars, that I couldn't help wondering about the mysteries of the universe.

The old skipper opened the door. After taking off our winter jackets and boots, we settled down in front of his glowing woodstove.

"Any news, guys?" Thomas started, handing us a mug of his famous cranberry tea.

"They hide boxes in the bunkers," I answered. "They're probably smugglers."

"That's a possibility," Thomas puffed on his pipe.

I hate the smell of cigarette smoke, but the sweet smell of pipe tobacco reminds me of other times. It made me think of the faraway places Thomas had visited years ago.

"We should have enough evidence now that those tourists are doing something illegal," Bas said.

Thomas nodded. "I did speak to some people and I found out where they're staying."

"Wow, Thomas. You missed your calling as a private investigator," I laughed.

"Who knows, if we get more criminal visitors on the island, I might have a future in that area," he chuckled.

"First thing this morning I went to the ferry. Sure enough, the brown station wagon you described to me was in the parking lot. There was nobody waiting in the car this time."

"All three of them had gone to the mainland to get more stuff?" I interrupted.

"Right," Thomas nodded. "All three of them came down the gangplank. The woman carried a blue suitcase. The men each carried a large sports bag. When they were loading their luggage in the trunk, I talked to one of the crew members and asked if he'd seen these people regularly on the ferry."

I hunched forward on my chair.

"The man told me he'd seen them. Sometimes two of them and some days all three go to the mainland, but he said the first couple of times there were *four* of them. The fourth person was a young man with short, reddish-blond hair and a big mouth, he said."

I trembled. "The body on the beach was that of a man with short, reddish-blond hair."

Bas nodded. "Maybe they had to get rid of the guy."

"But why would they leave him out on the beach?" I said. "If they had taken him directly to the bunker, or killed him there, we wouldn't have stumbled onto him. And Ice-woman would have never seen us down on the beach." It didn't make sense. By now I was convinced the woman on the dune had not been the ghost of Rixt, but Ice-woman, and that she, with the help of the two men, had moved the body away before we returned with Thomas.

"Don't get carried away now," Thomas said. "When the station wagon left the pier, I saw them turn right just before Nes. I followed the road to Buren and walked into the supermarket. I described the three tourists to the girl at the cash register and asked if she'd seen the three people in the store."

"Did she recognize them from your description?" Bas asked.

Thomas nodded. "The girl said they've been in the store on a regular basis to buy groceries and that they always ask for cardboard boxes."

"Aha, another clue," I looked around for a piece of

paper and a pencil.

"On the counter," Thomas pointed.

I picked up the note pad with the information Thomas had written out Monday night. "But did you find out where they live?"

"Yes, I did." Thomas puffed out a big cloud of smoke. "The girl thought they might be staying in Hotel East Dunes. She said she'd seen their brown station wagon in the parking lot. Next, I bicycled in the direction of Hotel East Dunes and sure enough, parked in the parking lot stood the station wagon. The Asian man was unloading luggage."

"What will we do next? Tell the police?" I jotted down all the information we had so far.

"Tomorrow after school we better pay Officer Kiewiet another visit," Thomas answered. "I'll meet you at the police station at four. And now the two of you should be on your way before Rikst gets grounded," he smiled.

•••

We made it home just in time. "I'll see you tomorrow, Bas."

"Yes, see you and good luck on your history test." Bas disappeared around the back of his house.

"So, did Thomas have interesting ideas for your story?" Dad winked.

"Yeah, but I won't use them." I blew my nose so I didn't have to look at my dad. But, of course he knew that it was only an excuse.

"Well, shall I type your story, tomorrow, or haven't you made up your mind yet?" Mom called from the dining room.

"I'll look it over one last time and I'll let you know." Just then the phone rang. "If it's Boukje, can I talk to her first?" Dad handed me the phone.

"Hi, how's it going, sis?" I dropped down in the antique chair beside the phone. "I guess you want to know about the three strange people first, before you want to know about me?"

"That's not true, but yes, it is kind of important."

"Okay," Boukje took her time. "All three were on the boat and they didn't really act all that suspicious, except for one thing."

"What, what was it?" I tried to keep my voice down.

"The woman was kissing the guy with the scar."

"Oh, gross! Well, I wasn't really interested in that," I answered.

"But that's not all, my sister, the investigator. The Asian guy looked angry. He balled his fists and walked away."

"And then," I asked. "What else did they do?"

"Nothing," Boukje answered. "In the harbor the three of them climbed into a taxi. Sorry to disappoint you."

"It's okay," I said. "How did your pictures of the gas rigs turn out?"

"They turned out really clear. But can you call Mom for me? I need to speak to her. It's important."

After handing the phone to Mom, I went upstairs to look at my essay. Covering my ears with the headphones of my Walkman, I listened to music and read once more the story of the witch of the bird sanctuary. After I'd put the story away, I opened my history book to the French Revolution and the time of Napoleon.

.11.

"Here it is, Mom." I placed the story beside her break-fast plate. "I hope you can read my scribbles." My hand shook. It felt like I was giving her my diary to read. But Mom always did a much better typing job than I and she was fast. Wednesday night I had weighed the pros and cons of letting Mom type my story. The pros won, because I can only type with two fingers.

"I'm sure I'll have no problem reading it," Mom leafed through the pages. "Thanks, Mom, I hope you don't find it a stupid story. I didn't stay with the facts too much."

"I thought you said you could stretch the facts to make it into a story," Mom looked at me seriously. "Don't worry about what I think," she said hoarsely.

I waited, hoping she would continue, but as usual she stayed silent. Rain splashed against the window panes. I reached for my slicker and stepped into my rubber boots.

"Good luck on your history test," Mom called as I left.

•••

"Hi, Rikst." Dirk parked his bicycle in the bike rack beside mine. "Did you finish your story yet?"

Puzzled, I looked at him. No mockery today, just a se-rious question. My face flushed. I felt more comfortable when he teased me. Now, I didn't know how to react.

"Lost your tongue, Rikst?" he smiled. He had a nice smile. I was still staring at him when he said, "I finished my story last night. It was interesting to research the history of my family. My father helped me. Over the years, he kept track of all the ups and downs of the company and now he wants to write a book about it."

I nodded. Why was he so friendly?

"Did you know that my dad and your mom used to date each other?"

"No," I shook my head in disbelief. My mom and Dirk's dad? The bell rang and brought me out of the sense of shock I felt. I hurried to my locker without looking back, knowing that Dirk was right behind me. I could feel his eyes in my back and see the smug grin on his face. When I walked into the room, history class was about to start.

"What were you and Dirk talking about?" Marijke asked when I sat down beside her. "Was he teasing you again?"

"No. It was so funny. He told me all about his own research and short story."

"What? I don't understand. Does that mean he's stopped calling you witch?"

"I don't know," I sighed. I didn't understand it either. His new behavior did make me feel confused. I didn't tell Marijke about Dirk's dad and my mom. Maybe he had made it up. But why would he do that? I shook my head and concentrated on the history test questions, which had already been handed out. I realized that my mind hadn't been on history the last few days. There were at least ten multiple-choice questions to which I had to guess the answers.

At lunch time there was no sign of Dirk in the cafeteria and I wondered if he'd left. Stop thinking about the guy, I disciplined myself.

•••

At four, Bas and I met with Thomas in front of the police station. Officer Kiewiet opened the door and smiled when he recognized the three of us. "Come in," he said. "I hope you didn't find more dead people on the beach?"

"No, not yet," Thomas answered and we followed the officer into the office.

"Have a seat and tell me what I can do for you."

"You start, Rikst," Thomas pointed at me, "and we'll fill in with the details."

"It all started with the dead body, officer," I began. And then I tried to recap all the events that had happened during the last week and a half. Officer Kiewiet took notes and Bas and Thomas added the information I left out.

"I think they're drug smugglers or something," I ended my account.

Officer Kiewiet rubbed his chin. He watched our faces. "Well, I must say you sure are onto something. But I can't do anything on my own. This time of year, I'm the only police officer on the island. Before I do anything to follow up on your story, I have to phone head office on the mainland and ask for assistance."

He looked as if he didn't really feel like getting involved in a job this size.

"How about Interpol, the International Criminal Police Organization?" Thomas asked. "Wouldn't that organization have the authority to arrest these people? They are foreigners and must have connections on the mainland. For instance, if we assume that they do indeed smuggle drugs, or weapons, they must get their loot on the mainland. The police need to trace which country supplies them."

"Yes. Yes." Officer Kiewiet nodded. He closed his

eyes for a second and tapped his fingers on the desk. So much for his quiet job on the island, I thought. Besides a sporadic speeding ticket and a brawl at the local bar on Saturday nights, there wasn't much excitement for a police officer in the wintertime.

"I'll make some phone calls," he said finally. "In the meantime, don't do anything that might endanger your lives. People who deal in drugs are always dangerous. And they probably carry weapons."

A shiver crept up my spine. When we spied on them at the bunkers, Bas and I had been so close to them.

"Yes, we'll be careful," Thomas said. He stood up. "I hope you'll let us know what happens next."

Officer Kiewiet rose from his chair, and Bas and I followed Thomas to the door.

"Thank you for all the information, and as I said before, don't get too close to these criminals."

"We won't," the three of us mumbled. We left the police station and pedaled down the street.

"Come to my place tomorrow night," Thomas said. "We'll decide what our next move is."

Bas and I bicycled home. There was no sign of the brown station wagon.

"I need to fix u1p my short story tonight," Bas said as he swung into his driveway.

"My mom had the day off, so she typed mine!" I called, before I entered through the back door to put my bike away for the night.

"Mmm, stew," I sniffed. "Stew with sausage. The perfect meal for this damp bone-chilling weather, Mom."

Mom didn't hear me. She still sat behind the computer in the dining room. I thought she would have typed my story first thing this morning.

"Can't you read my writing?" I asked when I walked into the room.

She looked up from the screen. "Yes, I mean no. I

have no trouble reading it." Her eyes misted as she looked at me.

"What's wrong, Mom? Is it my story?"

She shook her head. "No. It's just that … It's good. You wrote a good story."

I swallowed hard. I hadn't expected her to say that. Could my story have stumbled upon something to do with the reason I was named after Rixt from the bird sanctuary? Mom's face was flushed.

"You're right, Rikst. She wasn't only a witch, she was also a mother, no matter what the people say about her, or the horrible things she might have done. She was lonely — and a mother."

The back door slammed. Dad's entry disturbed the moment. Mom got up from the chair and walked into the kitchen to check on dinner. I still stood in the same spot and didn't hear what she and dad were talking about. I heard her set the table, but my mind stayed on my mother's words. She'd felt the same way about Rixt as I did. It made me feel good, but I was also intrigued by the question why. She must have had a good reason for naming me after the witch. Not just because she felt that Rixt was also a mother.

All through supper I thought about it. I wished Dad hadn't come in. Perhaps Mom would have said more. Give her time, Dad had asked me that day on the beach. She'll tell you, but she has to be ready. For the first time, I thought about Mom's feelings. Maybe she did carry a big secret that had something to do with Rixt from the bird sanctuary.

"Tired, ladies?" Dad broke the silence at the supper table. "You two have hardly said a word tonight, and I have the feeling Rikst hasn't even tasted the food she ate."

"Tell us about your day," Mom said in a forced voice.

Dad gave an account of his work in the dunes, but my mind went back to what Dirk had said this morning. My mother and his father ... I looked at my mom. Her face was delicate and oval-shaped with prominent cheek bones. Unlike me, she had a small straight nose, and full lips. Her eyes often shone dark and serious, but when she smiled her face was transformed and you could call it pretty. Perhaps she had smiled more when she was young, and maybe Dirk's handsome father had fallen for her smile. I sighed. I really couldn't ask Mom about that. She probably wouldn't want to talk about it. Maybe Dad didn't even know. When he was ten, he'd moved away from the island and hadn't returned until he was in his early twenties.

After supper I went upstairs. Without switching on the light, I sat down at my desk, rested my chin on the palms of my hands and stared out the window into the dark night. On the ceiling the shadows of branches, from the streetlights behind our neighbors, moved back and forth as if reaching for me. I closed my eyes. So many things had happened in the last few weeks. I felt I was on an emotional roller coaster. The story of Rixt, the smugglers, Mom's secret and then, this morning, Dirk's strange behavior. His nice smile had given me the shivers. Brrrr.

After turning on the desk lamp, I pulled my diary out of the bottom drawer. I kept the tiny key in a small compartment in my jewelry box. Unlocking the small book, I smoothed the pages. I flipped through the last two weeks. My eye caught the words "I hate Dirk. I hate the guy," several times.

Thursday, December 11

Dear Friend,

I don't know what's wrong with me. I feel confused. I will admit that since Dirk is acting differently, my feelings of hate for him have vanished. My thoughts returned to his conversation again and again today because I was too stunned to say anything. Just imagine my mom and his dad dating each other.

I was afraid if I opened my mouth he could hear my heart pounding. Dear friend, don't say anything. Don't judge me. I'm not going to fall for him like all the other girls. So even you, my friend, have to keep this secret locked up. I didn't mention it to Marijke because she has a crush on Dirk or as she says, "He's the guy I will compare every future boyfriend to." What a stupid idea. I still think he's arrogant and I hope that after a good night's sleep I will act normal again. I refuse to behave like most girls in my class.

And then, dear paper friend, there is my mom. I really don't know what to think anymore. But, for the first time, today I realize that there is more to my name than I had initially thought.

Of course, you would like to know about the three smugglers. We won't have much cooperation from Officer Kiewiet; therefore, we might do something about it. Don't worry. We won't catch them ourselves, but the three of us might do some closer investigation over the weekend. It seems that Thomas is really enjoying himself playing detective for Scotland Yard or Interpol. I find it exciting, as well, but I do worry sometimes how dangerous these people really are. Officer Kiewiet is convinced they have weapons; that's why he doesn't go near them. I don't know, except that I think Ice-woman is cold-blooded. Perhaps she killed the fourth man. Tomorrow I'll tell you about our plans for the weekend. My instincts warn me it's not going to be a quiet one.

Goodnight, dear friend.

For the rest of the evening I stayed in my room. I had no energy for homework. My mind was filled with thoughts of many different things: the three smugglers, my mom and her secret, and what Dirk had said about his dad and my mom. The last was the thing that really had me baffled. I found it so hard to imagine … Dirk's father and my mother. And I knew I couldn't ask Mom about it, no matter how much I wanted to.

.12.

At breakfast Mom handed me the printed copy of my short story. She told me I needed a brown envelope. Dad had left early and I hoped Mom would talk. But instead, she went to the dining room and found an envelope for me.

"I'm going to take a shower because I have some errands to do before I go to the museum today. Have a great day and I'll see you at supper." She walked upstairs and left me alone in the kitchen.

I quickly made my lunch; a peanut butter sandwich, an apple, a raisin bun and yogurt. As I stuffed everything into my backpack, I stopped. A thought struck me. An image of the ghost of Rixt flashed through my mind. Rixt was standing on the dune on a stormy night, waving a light back and forth. What if Ice-woman acted like Rixt? I rolled my bike outside. My mind was spinning. That was it! That was how she signaled the boats. Perhaps fishing boats took the smuggled goods from the island to Ireland or England.

All morning my mind kept going in circles until Miss Oud startled me, "Rikst did I miss your short story? Everybody has handed theirs in except you!"

All students turned in their seats to stare at me. Color rushed to my face. As I reached for my backpack and the large brown envelope, my elbow slipped off the desk. Groping around inside my pack, I realized the envelope wasn't there. What the …

"I don't see it, Miss Oud. I was sure …"

"I don't see it either, Rikst de Bruin." Her eyes bore straight into mine.

I frantically tried to think what I had done with my story. The last I remembered seeing it was when Mom handed me the envelope.

"Can I check my locker?" I asked.

"If you think you left it there. Go ahead."

Tripping over my legs, I stumbled out of my desk and headed for the hallway. When I had almost reached my locker, the sound of footsteps made me turn. It was Dirk.

"What are you doing here?" I asked.

"I came to help you find your story."

"I don't believe you. You came to say something mean."

"No, Rikst. I came to help you." His face looked earnest.

With my heart beating in my throat, I turned away from him and fumbled with the lock. My mind couldn't remember the proper combination. I took a deep breath and closed my eyes. I turned towards Dirk, looked straight in his eyes and shouted, "Get lost!"

He didn't move. "Open your locker, Rikst. Is it in there or not?" he asked quietly.

I shook my head. "It's at home." I managed to open the locker, took out my jacket.

"You want me to … "

"Don't even try." I hissed between clenched teeth. I turned away, left the building and Dirk.

Anger shook my body. I could hardly breathe. The nerve that guy had, to follow me out of the classroom. I wondered what the other students were thinking. Linda and her gang must have had a fit.

Turning into our driveway, I headed straight for the

workshop. I must have left it on Dad's workbench when I took my bike. It wasn't there either. Underneath a terra-cotta flower pot, we hid a house key. I opened the door to the kitchen. The breakfast table had been cleared. My story wasn't on the kitchen counter either. I checked the dining room and upstairs, but no brown envelope. Pulling out a chair, I sat down at the kitchen table. What was I supposed to do next? I couldn't face Miss Oud. She'd kill me with her looks.

Mom. The phone. I dialed the number of the museum, but there was no answer. I re-dialed the number every ten minutes for the next half hour, but without luck. Either Mom was on her lunch break or she wasn't answering the phone. After one last try, I left the house and bicycled in the direction of the museum. From a distance, I spotted the CLOSED sign in the window.

Defeated, I pedaled back to school. I would have to reprint my story tonight and deliver it to Miss Oud in person. With my head down, I walked to my locker. In that posture, I didn't see Mom waiting for me.

"Were you looking for this?" Mom held out a brown envelope to me.

Startled, I looked up. " Yes! Thanks, Mom. Where did you find it?"

"When I checked the workshop before I left this morning, I found it lying on the floor."

"I thought I'd lost it!"

"It's still in the computer," Mom smiled. "We could have printed another copy. You better go. Miss Oud probably wonders where you are. See you tonight."

"Bye, Mom and thanks."

The rest of the morning went without obstacles, even though Miss Oud frowned at me for the remainder of class.

•••

After school I waited for Bas outside.

"Why aren't you coming with me?" Marijke asked.

"Oh, sorry, Marijke. I completely forgot that I was going to the hairdresser with you. Do you mind if I don't come this time? Bas and I have a few errands to do."

"Fine," Marijke said sarcastically. "You haven't been much fun lately, anyway. You're either with Bas or Dirk. Call me when you can find the time to spend with me."

My face burned. "That's not fair. I haven't been with Dirk at all. For your information, I can't stand the guy. So don't worry. You can have him."

Marijke stood still holding onto her bike. I felt awful. We hardly ever quarreled. Why did I say all these terrible things to her?

"I'll call you tonight," I said softly.

Marijke turned and left the school yard.

"Wow," Bas' voice sounded right behind me. "I thought the two of you never fought."

"We don't. Not until today. And I feel bad. It's my fault. I haven't been honest with her lately. I haven't told her anything about our discovery."

And I didn't tell her about my feelings for Dirk, I thought. But I couldn't share that with Bas either. He wouldn't understand. He thought girls were insane to fall for Dirk.

"Let's go to Thomas'," I said.

It was a lovely afternoon for December. The sky was clear and the air crisp. The wind blew hair in my face. The salty scent of the sea and the cries of the gulls that rode the wind currents above our heads soon allowed me to forget the argument with my friend.

Thomas was waiting for us outside his cottage. We followed him inside. As always the smell of his tobacco, cranberry tea and freshly baked raisin buns welcomed us.

"Sit down, guys. Let's get to business. We have a crime

to solve," he chuckled. His eyes gleamed; I got the feeling that he was really enjoying this adventure.

"Did you find out more about the smugglers?" I asked.

"Yes," Thomas answered. "This morning I went to the parking lot of Hotel East Dunes and watched the brown station wagon. At about ten, all three of them left the building carrying grocery boxes."

"More drugs or whatever," Bas said.

"I couldn't follow the car, of course, but I suspect they headed for the bunkers. What I'd really like to find out is where they take the stuff from there?"

I could hardly wait to tell what I thought. This morning it had come to me in a flash, just like that.

"They bring stuff from the mainland to the island and hide it in the bunkers," Bas pulled on his sleeves. "How can we find out what they do with it? Unless it is stolen goods and they want to get rid of it."

"That's another possibility," Thomas said. "Assuming they have drugs, they have to take that stuff somewhere. Where would they go next? We can't possibly guard the bunkers twenty-four hours a day."

My feet moved restlessly on the wooden floor. The palms of my hands were damp. "This morning I got an idea," I said. "It's probably stupid."

"Let's hear it," Thomas encouraged. Bas nodded.

"Remember how I saw Ice-woman on top of the dunes the day we found the body?"

They both nodded.

"If Ice-woman knows the legend of Rixt from the bird sanctuary, then she knows that people on the island are superstitious and believe that Rixt's ghost wanders through the dunes in stormy weather."

"But I don't see the connection between Ice-woman and Rixt," Thomas said.

"I think Ice-woman acts like Rixt. She stands on a

dune at night and signals boats to pick up the drugs." I looked around the table.

Thomas' eyes lit up. Bas' showed admiration.

"You got it, Rikst, old girl. It's a bit far-fetched, but, you could be right," Thomas said.

"How will we find out?" Bas stood up from his chair. "We can't patrol the whole beach, and we don't know when they are going to signal the boats."

"You're right, Bas. But we could try," Thomas said.

"The place where we found the body might be the spot where they transfer the drugs to fishing boats," I said.

"That's a good start," Thomas said. "And which nights they ship their loot, we just have to guess. How about tomorrow night? The two of you can stay here with me. Just bring your sleeping bags."

"I hope I'm allowed," I sighed. "These days, Mom makes a big deal out of everything. I wish she was more like your mom, Bas. Your mom is so easygoing. She never fusses."

Bas shrugged.

"Tomorrow night will be an excellent night for star-gazing," Thomas winked. "We might not see anything, but it's worth a try. Are the two of you game?"

We nodded in agreement.

"Time to go, kids." Thomas stood up and we followed him out the door.

The evening sky was still clear. When I looked up, I saw a million stars shining down on us. Tomorrow night might indeed be a good night for stargazing. I smiled.

. 13 .

Boukje didn't come home for the weekend. She stayed with a friend on the mainland. I missed her and it was going to be a long Saturday and Sunday, except for to-night. Mom had actually given permission for me to stay over at Thomas'. I couldn't believe it. She didn't even question me. Mom looked pale with dark circles under her eyes. When I looked at her, she gave me a thin smile.

"I'm all right, Rikst. I haven't slept very well. You and I have to talk soon."

My heart skipped. "I have time today," I said quickly. "And I don't want you to have sleepless nights over it."

"No, I have to do groceries and finish the present for Saakje. Tomorrow is their silver wedding anniversary and I still have to paint one last coat of varnish on the oak frame. After the weekend we'll find some time together."

"Okay," I sighed. "I'll phone Marijke and see what she is up to today."

There was no answer at Marijke's. By the time I finished re-dialing, Mom had left to do groceries and Dad had gone to play squash with his friend Jan. Funny that Dad's best friend and Mom's best friend were married to each other and tomorrow was their anniversary. They had organized a big party — but for adults only — so tomorrow was going to be a long one too. Not that I wanted to go to the party. It probably would be boring with people sitting around, eating and drinking. At night friends would perform skits and jokes to entertain the couple. No, I wouldn't miss it. I just wished Boukje was home. I felt restless.

Just before lunch I decided to visit Bas and his mom. Aunt Anna opened the door. Her hair was tied in a ponytail and she wore her paint smock, which meant she was probably working on an assignment. I followed her into the studio. In the corner stood her easel. A low table with palettes of paint stood against the wall. The watercolor on the easel portrayed the lighthouse.

"It's really good, Aunt Anna. I love how you use the blues for the sky and the sea. But they are so different. The sea is so alive. The sky is a real summer sky."

"Well, thank you," she smiled. "This one has to be completed by next Friday. A company on the mainland wants to hang it in their new office building. Did you like the one I did for your mom's friend?"

"Yes, Saakje will love the wild flowers you painted. The soft pastel colors of the petals bring the flowers to life. Mom has to put one more coat of varnish on the frame today."

"Let's go into the kitchen and make hot chocolate. Bas is in the workshop," Aunt Anna said.

I followed her into the kitchen. "I'll get Bas."

"I don't think he wants you to see what he's working on. I'll call him."

Why would Bas not show me? Perhaps he wanted his project finished before he showed it to me. I shrugged my shoulders.

"Hi, Rikst," Bas entered the kitchen. "Bored without your sister?"

"Yes. Mom's doing groceries and Dad's playing squash."

"Do you want to go to the west end after lunch?"

"Sure. If I can't get a hold of Marijke. I promised I'd call her today."

"Yes, you better make up with her. She was angry yesterday." Bas snickered.

"It's not funny, Bas. I treated her badly. She didn't deserve that."

After drinking hot chocolate in their cozy kitchen, I went back home and tried phoning Marijke once more. I made myself a peanut butter sandwich for lunch. At one I returned to Bas' house with my bike.

The sky was overcast and the wind from the west froze my fingers around the handlebars. As before we parked our bicycles at the lighthouse.

"Did you plan to go back to the bunkers?" I asked.

"Yes, let's go," Bas motioned in the direction of the conservation area.

"Don't you think they can see us easily during the day?" I followed Bas through the rosehip and hawthorn bushes.

"We can't go as close to the bunkers as during the night. But we'll find a spot," Bas convinced me.

When we neared the shelters, we stooped over and crawled on our hands and knees.

"There's nobody there, as far as I can see," Bas looked back at me. I followed closely. The thorns scratched my face and hands as we neared the barbed wire fence. Slowly, we crawled to the north side of the bunker.

"Down on your stomach!" Bas whispered. "They're here!"

I felt the heat of danger crawl over my body. My hands felt damp. What were they doing at the bunkers today?

We stayed on our stomachs beneath a rosehip bush. We were both breathing unevenly.

"Look," I pointed. "They're taking the boxes out of

the bunker."

"Do you know what that means?" Bas asked.

"Tonight might be the night they are going to get rid of their goods."

Bas nodded. We watched how Ice-woman, the Irishman and the little Asian guy carried boxes from the bunker, through the fence and up the dune.

"The station wagon must be on the other side of the dune," I said.

Bas nodded. "Watch. The Irishman dropped a small package from the box. It fell into those bushes over there."

I followed Bas' finger, but I didn't see the package. The Irishman didn't notice it either. The three of them came back. They looked around and stopped. Would they spot us now? After a few seconds, the big one pulled a lock out of his pocket and snapped it on the door. The three of them left through the hole in the fence and disappeared in the bushes. I slowly released my breath.

"We have to get the package," I told Bas.

"Let's wait a few minutes," he said. "Then you go to the top of the dune and keep watch, while I go through the fence and get the package. I sure don't want to be caught in there if they come back."

I nodded. My heart beat wildly in my chest. I didn't feel the cold any more. We waited. The strong wind meant we could not hear the sound of the engine. After three or four minutes we decided that they must have left. Then we moved quickly. I climbed cautiously up the dune. When I neared the top, I slid onto my stomach and peered over the edge. Down below I could see the tire tracks in the sand, but there was no station wagon. We were counting on the fact that all three of them had left. But what if one of them had stayed behind? He or she could surprise us any minute. I heard a rustling sound behind me. I froze, unable to draw a breath.

"I've got it," Bas whispered. He held out the package for me to see. It was the size of a small brick and wrapped in heavy brown paper and taped at the ends.

"Quickly. Let's get out of here," he said.

We slid down the dune and crawled through the bushes.

"We better go this way," I pointed to the south side of the bunkers.

We stayed as low as possible and followed the fence around the bunker.

"Stop!" I put my hand on Bas' arm. "What's that?"

Next to the concrete wall of the bunker was a small mound of freshly turned sand. Where the sand had been dug up the marram grass had been removed. The bare patch was about two meters long and less than one wide.

"It's a grave!" I whispered. I kept my trembling hand on Bas' arm. "It's the grave of the man we found on the beach. I'm sure it is. Let's get out of here. It's creepy!"

Hearts pounding, we reached our bicycles. Bas stuffed the package in the front of his jacket.

"You want to open it?" I asked.

"No. We should take it to Officer Kiewiet." He jumped on his bike and set off in the direction of Nes.

I followed as if someone was chasing after us. Bas was scared too I thought. Although he would never admit it.

We pedaled hard all the way and, though the wind was behind us, we were both gasping for breath when we arrived at the police station. Bas rang the bell. We waited.

"Ring again," I urged.

Nothing happened. Bas tried the door, but it was locked. Frustration in his eyes, he looked at me.

"Thomas," I said. "Let's ask him what to do."

In silence we bicycled to the old skipper's cottage. Bas knocked. No one answered and the door was locked. Defeated, we looked at each other.

"Let's go to the beach," I suggested. I needed to feel the wind around my head. Hear the sound of the waves. Feel the sand beneath my feet. Taste the salt on my lips. There, close to the waves, surrounded by nature, I could clear my mind and sort out the problems we'd met this afternoon.

We walked in silence to the eastern tip of the island, where no one ever went. The heather was brown and lifeless. In the late summer this area was beautiful, a mass of violet. I saw in Bas' face the same struggle that I felt. Had we gone too far? Would it not be better to leave all of this to the police? This was beginning to look like something too serious for an old skipper and two teenagers. What had begun as an adventure suddenly seemed like much more than we had bargained for. I sighed.

"Bas." I touched his arm.

Bas took his hand from his pocket. "I'm scared, Rikst. I'm afraid to know what's in the package."

"Shall we open it?" I wasn't sure that I really wanted to know what was in the package either. But my curiosity was too strong. Surely it couldn't hurt to look. "Let's go into the shelter of the dune over there and take a look."

"What if it contains explosives?" Bas said.

That possibility hadn't occurred to me. I was thinking it would be white powder. Drugs. The kind of thing I'd seen in movies on television.

"All right," he nodded.

We sat down in the shelter of the dune, out of the wind. The clouds chased each other overhead. Bas took the package from his coat. He weighed it in his hand. My eyes followed his motions.

"About a kilogram," Bas estimated. With his pocket-knife he slit the tape at one end. Carefully, he folded the paper down. I think now we were both thinking about explosives. He turned the package on end so that we could peek in to the opening he had made. But all we saw was red cellophane. There was another layer to the packaging.

Bas looked at his knife; then at me. I shook my head.

He sucked in his breath, paused and said, "The drugs are inside."

I nodded. My mouth was too dry to talk.

"Maybe we shouldn't open it," Bas said. "The stuff might blow away. If we lose the evidence, we've got nothing."

"We could open it at Thomas'." The words came out in a whisper.

"It would be even better if we let Officer Kiewiet open it," Bas answered. "Then he'll have to believe us."

"Okay," I stood up and wiped the sand from my jeans and parka. My curiosity had disappeared; now I felt only a rising tension. Fear. "Let's go back to Thomas', but after that, I have to go home. If Thomas still isn't back, you should bring the package with you tonight."

Bas followed me back to the skipper's cottage. The seagulls swooped down low over our heads. We were the only people on the beach. When we found the cottage still unoccupied, we bicycled home. Nearing the end of Sand Dike, a brown car approached from the village.

I turned my head and yelled at Bas, "It's them!"

"Keep going," Bas shouted.

The station wagon came at us. A cloud of dirt sprayed out behind it like a parachute. My heart beat in my throat. The driver didn't leave any room on the narrow road for us. Did he not see us?

"Jump!" Bas cried.

Without thinking, I wheeled into the shrubs beside

the road. Head first, I crashed into the branches and crumpled to the ground on top of my bike. I lay there stunned by what had happened. Then it dawned on me that Bas might be hurt. I untangled myself from my bike and the bushes and got up.

As I got back out onto the roadway, Bas appeared from a neighboring shrub. Sand and sticks covered his hair.

"Are you hurt?" I watched how he rubbed the back of his head.

"They were trying to kill us!" his voice quivered.

All I could do was nod my head. My knees felt weak and my stomach queasy.

"Are you all right, Rikst?"

I looked in Bas' white face and nodded. "How about you?"

"I'm fine, I think. Let's go."

As we pedaled the rest of the way into the village, we didn't speak, each of us trying to come to terms with the strange events we had witnessed that afternoon. When we arrived at Bas' driveway, we stopped and stood facing each other in the fading light.

"Tonight could be dangerous. Are you sure you want to go?" Bas asked.

"Yes," I replied, with more confidence than I felt. "I think we'll be safe with Thomas."

"Is seven okay with you then?"

"Yes." Then I whispered, "Bas, what about the package?"

"Don't worry. My mom won't find it."

.14.

With our sleeping bags secured to our backpacks, Bas and I rode out of the village, but not before we had stopped at the police station. And again the place was locked. Officer Kiewiet was nowhere in sight.

"What do people do in an emergency?" I said.

"I don't know. Maybe you have to go to the fire station instead."

I shook my head. As we reached the outskirts of the village, I pulled over to the side of the road. "I don't want to risk meeting the station wagon again," I said. "Let's take the sand trail to Thomas' cottage."

"You're right," Bas led the way over the dune.

I followed him along the trail through rosehip bushes and other prickly shrubs. Sometimes we had to carry our bikes when the sand was too loose.

The night was cold and the moonless sky still cloudy. Our plans for stargazing had gone astray. But Mom and Dad hadn't said anything during supper. Plowing through the sand, I remembered Mom's words about our having a talk soon. Had she changed her mind after reading my short story? Would the mystery of my name be cleared up? The wind rose and sand whipped in our faces.

"This is hard, Bas," I called.

"Hard, but safe," he answered.

Despite the cold temperatures, I perspired beneath

my winter jacket. I was worried about what we were getting ourselves into. I was glad Thomas would be with us. I knew that he had been through his fair share of dangerous situations during his life as a ship's captain.

We were relieved when we finally saw the lights of Thomas' cottage.

"Come in, guys," he opened the door and gently pulled us inside.

Bas took the package inside his coat and placed it on the table.

"What's that?" Thomas studied the small parcel.

"The smugglers lost it this afternoon near the bunker," the words rushed out. My breath came fast, both from apprehension and the workout we'd just had.

"Did you check what's inside?"

"We opened it partly," Bas said, "but then decided we should take it to Officer Kiewiet. But the police station was closed. Inside the brown paper is red cellophane. We think there are drugs inside the cellophane."

"We didn't open it because we were afraid the powder, if it is drugs, might blow away." I shifted uncomfortably on my chair. "They loaded the parcels from the bunker into their station wagon. And tonight we met them on Sand Dike. They tried to drive us off the road. They tried to kill us." I looked at Bas. He nodded.

"Wow," Thomas shook his head in disbelief. "It looks like they're getting worried. We might be right on top of them tonight."

I felt a lump in my throat. Was it okay to do this? This was dangerous.

"Let's have a look inside," Thomas continued. With a jackknife he took from his pocket he made a small incision in the red cellophane. White powder showed through the slit. Thomas lifted a small amount on the blade of the knife. He raised it to his nose. Then he carefully wet the tip of one finger and gently touched it to the blade. He then touched the tip of his finger to his tongue.

"I've seen them do that on the television," he laughed, breaking the tension that we felt. "It has a very bitter taste. I think it's heroin. Likely from Asia."

Tiny beads of perspiration trickled down Thomas' forehead. He wiped them off with the sleeve of his sweater. My head swam. What had we gotten ourselves into? Officer Kiewiet was right when he said these people might be armed and dangerous. If they were transporting the drugs tonight, they didn't want any onlookers.

"What's next, Thomas?" I asked.

"We'll dress warmly and go out to the place where you found the body. Except we can't go down on the beach," Thomas answered. "We're lucky it's a dark night. We won't bring any flashlights. Or would the two of your rather leave things as they are and just take the package to the police station, so Officer Kiewiet can figure it out."

"No, I want to go," I said.

"Me, too," Bas nodded.

"Then let's get ready." Thomas took his sweater from the back of a chair and pulled it over his head. "We better bring something to eat. It might be a long night. And here is an old blanket." He pulled a rolled-up blanket from a shelf. From the kitchen drawer, he took a piece of rope and tied it around the blanket. "Here, Bas, you hang on to that."

Rummaging through his cupboards, Thomas packed some buns and three apples in a bag. "You are in charge of the food, Rikst." I stuffed the food in my backpack. Next, the old skipper found a large, black umbrella, which he could use for a walking stick. "Just in case we get some rain, tonight." He left the lights on in the cottage and locked the door. We were on our way. We followed Thomas, who knew the way through the dunes with his eyes closed.

At first I staggered over clumps of sand; later, my eyes adjusted to the darkness and I could make out the shadows of the bushes in contrast to the white sand. At one point I stumbled and almost fell into a bush. I yelped as I startled a hare out of its lair.

"Sorry, guys," I panted.

"It's all right," Thomas had turned around to wait for me. "We might want to cross over to the last dune and have a peek at the beach," he said. "But stay low. We don't want to be seen."

Climbing to the top of the dune made me warm. I started sweating in my wool sweater and winter jacket. I pulled off the hood and the wind blew my hair in my face and eyes. When I tried to brush the strands away with the back of my hand, sand flew in my eyes. I stopped and closed them.

"Do you need help?" Bas had crawled down the dune to check what took me so long.

"No. I just got sand in my eyes, that's all."

"You're almost there."

"Come on, guys," Thomas called softly.

"He must see something," I said. I forgot about the sand and crawled behind Bas to the top of the dune.

"On your stomachs," Thomas said. We saw the shape of his outstretched body on the slope of the dune and we lay down beside him in the same position.

"Look out over the sea. No. More over there." In the dark I saw his arm pointing east.

"See those lights?"

"Yes," I said.

"That's a fishing trawler. It's not moving."

I focused my eyes on the bobbing lights in the distance. "Could they be putting the net out or hauling it in at this time of the night?" I asked.

"Not likely. Not in the dark," Thomas said.

Waves sloshed onto the beach. The tide was coming in. I could hear the breakers rolling and boiling in the distance. The wind swept the waves higher and higher as they splashed closer to the shore.

"There!" Bas said. "A signal. Look, the people on the boat are signaling."

Then I saw it. The beam of a light flashed three times. It stopped and flashed three times again.

"We should move more eastward," Thomas said. "We can't see what they're doing in the dunes from here."

My heart thumped loudly as I followed my two friends. I felt like I was in a movie, right in the part with all the action. Slowly, we crawled up and down the dunes.

"Stop." Thomas moved back. "We'd better stay on this side of the dune. They are right over there."

We crept around the west side of the dune and stayed on our stomachs. I still hadn't seen the criminals.

"There she is. On top of the third dune." Thomas pointed to the east. I followed the direction his arm showed, but failed to see Ice-woman. "There's a black shadow on the third dune," Thomas repeated.

"Yes," Bas whispered. "It's Ice-woman."

I focused my eyes, again. Then, I saw her. My heart stopped. It was as if time stood still. I was back in the days when Rixt roamed the beaches and beckoned ships at night. I saw her standing on top of the dune. A dark cloak billowing in the wind. Her long, white hair blowing to one side. Next, I saw the light in her hand. She raised her arm and the light swung back and forth, back and forth, just as I had seen her in my dream.

"The ghost of Rixt," Thomas whispered.

"The witch of the bird sanctuary," Bas said.

"Ice-woman," I added.

With squinting eyes, the three of us observed the light in the dune.

"Watch," Bas pointed. "The ship is coming closer.

And look. Down on the beach!"

I followed the movement of Bas' arm. The lights in the distance came nearer. A small light broke away from the others. "It must be a dinghy," I said. The bigger vessel couldn't come any closer.

My eyes scanned the shoreline. Two figures were moving in the direction of the sea. By the way they walked we could tell that they each carried a load.

"Where would they have parked the car?" Bas said. "It can't be close to the dunes. There's no trail there."

"Perhaps they've been carrying the stuff out here since this afternoon," Thomas answered.

The lights bobbed up and down, up and down as the small boat rode through the breakers. "The dinghy's reached the beach." I tried to get more comfortable. My neck was sore from the strain.

We watched as two shadows jumped out of the small rubber boat and pulled it onto the beach. They began loading whatever it was the others had dumped on the beach, while our two smugglers went back to the dunes. Ice-woman had disappeared. I wished I could see her. I'd rather know where all three of them were. Hopefully, she wouldn't scan the area.

The Irishman and the Asian were soon back with another load. After that had been stowed in the dinghy, the other two pulled the boat back into the sea and returned to their vessel.

We waited. I shivered. My body had turned cold. I remembered the food in my backpack. Without speaking, I handed Thomas and Bas each a bun. Bas unrolled the blanket. We huddled closer together, and Bas tucked the cover around us. Nothing happened for a while. I turned on my back and watched the clouds, black shadows, fleeing to the east.

What feelings did Rixt have when she lured the ships at night? Was it her survival instinct or had greed taken over? She must have been so lonely after her son had gone to sea.

"They're back." Bas moved beside me.

In one swift movement, I rolled back onto my stomach and watched the two smugglers carry more boxes to the shoreline. There was no sign of Ice-woman.

"Here comes the dinghy," I pointed in the direction of the lights that were headed toward the beach.

We watched a second time as the rubber boat was loaded and then left again. After a while — was it ten minutes or fifteen, I'd lost track of time — the fishing boat gave another signal. Twice the light flashed. At that moment I saw Ice-woman. She'd returned to her spot on top of the dune and waved her light back and forth. She stood tall. The contours of her cape and head clearly outlined by the light in her hand.

"It must be their signal that their mission is completed," Thomas said. "We'll wait for a while and then we better head home to get some sleep. Where are those apples, Rikst?"

I reached in my backpack and handed Thomas and Bas each an apple. We moved down in the hollow of the dune, out of the wind. Bas checked his watch. Eleven-fifteen. We'd been in the dunes for three hours, although it hadn't felt that long. Fatigue crept into my legs. Slowly, the tension left my body.

Thomas climbed back to the top of the dune and scanned the area. "No sign of our three friends. The lights of the boat are moving away from the island," he said. "We should head home. Let's take our time. Be careful."

.15.

For several hours, I tossed and turned in my sleeping bag. My bedroom was in Thomas' attic, while Bas slept on the floor in the living room. We'd had this kind of sleepover occasionally for the last few years. When we first stayed over, I must have been ten. It was such an adventure. I remember Thomas telling us that he had caught a rat in his kitchen. That's when I had decided to take to higher grounds, even though I knew rats could climb into the attic as well.

When I finally fell asleep, I dreamed of a woman standing on top of the dune waving her light back and forth, calling my name. "Rikst! Rikst! You stole my name! My name! My name!"

The sound of rattling pots and pans woke me in the morning. A blue sky peeked through the small skylight in the attic. I watched a tiny, fluffy cloud sailing past. I lay there thinking of the events of last night. Muffled voices came from downstairs. Bas and Thomas were early risers; I wasn't. I sighed, yawned and unzipped my sleeping bag. I reached for my jeans and turtleneck, and dressed quickly. The air in the attic chilled my tired body. I straightened the bed, rolled up my sleeping bag and went down to the delicious smells of fried bacon and eggs, a delicacy we never ate at home.

"Morning, Rikst. Sleep well?" Thomas stood in front of the stove, flipping the bacon in the frying pan. Bas had set the table. A large piece of rye bread rested on each plate. The pot filled with cranberry tea sat over a warming candle in the center of the table.

"Morning. No, I had a bad dream about Rixt," I said. "She stood on top of the dune waving her light and calling, 'You stole my name!' "

"You still haven't found out why your parents named you after the witch?" Thomas turned around holding the frying pan. He scooped bacon onto our plates.

"No, but Mom said she'll tell me soon."

"She must have a good reason, Rikst," Thomas said. "Why else would she keep it from you? Perhaps you need to be old enough to understand."

"Yeah, maybe," I sighed, before I dug into my breakfast.

After helping Thomas clear the table, we set out to the village. We had decided that we would pay Officer Kiewiet a visit first thing.

The door to the police station was open. As we walked in, Thomas called Officer Kiewiet's name. We were barely inside when the door to his office opened and Officer Kiewiet, his face flushed, invited us in. To our surprise, we were not the only visitors on this early Sunday morning. Across from his desk sat two gentlemen in trench coats.

"Come in. I shall get some more chairs," the police officer bustled. He acted as if he'd expected us to show up this early on a Sunday morning.

"No. No. It's fine. We can stand. We won't take much of your time," Thomas spoke.

"This is Inspector de Boer and Inspector Jongsma from the mainland. They are detectives from Interpol, and have come to assist me in the case the three of you brought to my attention. Before we start, I must caution you not to repeat any of this conversation to anyone outside this building." With these words he straightened up in his chair and tried to look important. "Is that understood?"

All three of us nodded. There was no need to tell them that so far we had kept everything secret.

Wow! I was impressed. Officer Kiewiet had certainly gone into action after the last time we'd talked to him. Bas winked at me. He must have had the same thoughts.

We explained our new findings and answered many questions. The two trench coats wrote in their notebooks. They looked serious. Especially after Thomas placed the package on the desk. Inspector de Boer took the package, ripped off the tape, which Thomas had replaced, and shook a bit of the white powder into the palm of his hand. Just as Thomas had done, he too tasted a tiny bit of it on the moistened tip of his little finger. He nodded to his colleagues, as if to confirm their suspicions. Inspector Jongsma and Officer Kiewiet nodded in agreement.

"You can leave the rest of the investigation up to us," Inspector de Boer said. His face told us he didn't need or want our help.

Very shortly we were back out on the street.

"Well, that's it guys," Thomas said as he picked up his bicycle. "Our job is finished. The experts can catch them and lock them up. Thanks for bringing me some excitement."

We laughed. Some excitement, I thought. We quickly said our good-byes. Thomas set off for his cottage and we headed home.

"What will you do this afternoon?" Bas asked.

"Oh. If I'm in the mood, I might bake something. I'll see. And what about you?"

"I have an assignment to finish," he smiled.

"In the workshop? You're carving something out of that big piece of driftwood you found the other day, aren't you?"

"Keep guessing. I won't tell. It's a surprise."

"For me?"

"Yes, for you." Bas' eyes twinkled.

"I *love* surprises. But don't keep me waiting too long, or I might burst."

"Be patient. See you."

"See you."

I went straight to my room to write in my diary. Mom and Dad were already at their party. A note on the kitchen table told me there was lasagna in the fridge for supper.

I had a lot to think about. And I definitely wasn't in the mood for homework. After I closed and locked my diary, I lay down on my bed for a while. I felt tired. I was glad the adventure was over. I mean I was glad we were not chasing Ice-woman and her men anymore.

I must have dozed off, because when I looked at my watch again it was five-thirty. I had slept for four hours. My stomach growled and I went down to the kitchen to make a sandwich. I didn't feel like baking and went back upstairs. Opening my closet to check what I was going to wear tomorrow, I found one of Mom's shirts hanging beside mine. I took it out and walked into my parents' bedroom. Their room was bright and much bigger than mine. Mom had decorated the room in blue and white. I hung the blouse in her closet and walked over to the dresser. Several framed pictures of my sister and I were lined up on the top. They had all been taken when we were small. In a double frame Mom had put pictures of us when we were only a few days old. We didn't look alike at all. Boukje's head was bald, while I had black hair that stood straight on end. Boukje's face was round and chubby; mine was longer. My eyes were much darker than hers. Another picture showed Dad reading us a story with both of us sitting in his lap.

Beside the picture stood Mom's music box. I picked it up carefully. The two ivory swans had their heads back. A hairline crack showed where the neck had been broken, but it was hardly noticeable. The wooden music box had been given to my mom when she was ten by her great-grandmother. I opened the lid. I listened to the tune of 'Au clair de la lune,' while the swans twirled around and around. When I was little I always wanted to listen to this song. The music must have driven Mom crazy.

Without any purpose in mind I lifted the music box to look underneath. It was then that I noticed a tiny latch that secured a small door on the bottom of the box. I had never noticed this before. I flipped the latch and the door opened. As I turned the music box over to close the door again, I saw a white piece of paper inside the tiny compartment. Or was it cardboard? With my thumb and index finger I removed the paper. It was a photo, old and somewhat faded, but still clear. A picture of a newborn baby. There was no name on the picture. The baby had a long face and black hair sticking out. I gasped. Was it a picture of me? But why was it hidden in the music box?

I stared at the baby picture for a long time. I held it beside my own baby picture and even though I could see some resemblance between the two newborns, they were not identical. So it wasn't my baby picture. But who was it? We didn't have cousins our age. But why was it hidden in the music box?

Dusk fell and the shadows created by the streetlight made me shiver. With trembling fingers, I slipped the picture back into the compartment, closed the latch and placed the music box back on the dresser. Hastily, I backed out of the room. Apprehension filled my chest; I had invaded my mother's privacy.

I sat at my desk and stared out into the backyard. I sat that way for some time. Then the sound of the phone ringing made me jump. It was Mom checking to see how I was doing.

"Did you have fun at Thomas'?" she asked.

"Thomas? Oh, yes we did."

"Are you all right? You sound so distant."

"Yes, I'm fine, Mom. How is the party?"

"It's great. And they loved the painting. Make sure you eat something. We'll see you later. Bye."

"Bye, Mom." I looked at the receiver. How could Mom act so normal, while she had this secret picture of a newborn baby hidden in the compartment of her music box? I wondered if Dad knew about it.

I sighed and went to the kitchen to heat up the lasagna. Even though I felt hungry, Mom's cooking didn't taste as good as it usually did. After eating I went into the living room to close the curtains. Mom always wanted the curtains drawn so no one from the street could look in at night. I looked out at the quiet street. I was just reaching to pull the curtains closed when I noticed a car parked several houses down the street. Panic choked me. Was it … Stop, I warned myself. Every car parked in the street wasn't the brown station wagon. Besides they'd probably left the island now that the drugs had been handed over. The car was mostly in shadow so I couldn't make out its color. Then as I drew the last curtain, the headlights switched on. I watched through the crack between the curtains as a dark station wagon slowly passed our house. I froze and waited for the sound of the engine to return. I couldn't be sure that this was *the* brown station wagon — surely there were other dark-colored station wagons on the island! — but, just the same, I felt very apprehensive. When the car didn't come back, I left the living room. At first I thought of calling Bas and asking him to come over, but in the end I simply went upstairs to read and listen to music.

When my parents finally came home near midnight, I pretended to be asleep. But it took a long time before real sleep rescued me from my fears.

.16.

Marijke waited for me at the bicycle rack. Her pretty face forecast a storm. "I thought you were going to call me on the weekend?"

"I did. Saturday morning I tried to call you several times," I snapped back.

"When I wasn't there Saturday morning, you assumed I was gone for the whole weekend?"

"No. I didn't. I got busy in the afternoon."

"I thought you said you'd have a boring weekend with Boukje staying on the mainland and your parents going to the anniversary party?"

"Yes, but something else came up." I felt awful not being able to share any of my adventures with Marijke. But I had been told not to say anything. I couldn't involve her. And I was pretty sure she wouldn't understand.

"Care to tell me about your busy weekend?"

"No. I can't. I'm sorry."

"I'm sure you're sorry. If it has something to do with Dirk, I don't want to know."

"It has nothing to do with Dirk." I brushed my hair from my face and headed into the school. "I told you before, Marijke, you can have Dirk. There's nothing going on between us, except that he has stopped calling me witch. Maybe he got bored with it." I sighed and looked away. I didn't want to lose my best friend. But right now, it seemed there was nothing I could do to make things right between us.

"You wanna go for a coke after school?" I tried, as we arrived at our lockers.

"No, thanks. I have plans already." With that she headed down the hall to where Linda stood surrounded by her gang of faithful followers.

I fumbled with my backpack and books until the bell rang.

"Are you and Marijke fighting?"

Surprised, I looked at the handsome face peeking around the door of my locker. I flushed. "Hi. Yes."

"I'm sorry," Dirk said. "It looks pretty serious."

His eyes were sincere. I was surprised that he meant it.

"Yes," I said. "And it's all my fault." I don't know why I said that to him. "I hope I can make it up some day."

Dirk nodded. I avoided looking at his face for fear that he would notice my red cheeks.

"So. Look at this, girls. Who do we have here?"

I turned around and faced the group of girls glaring at us. It was Linda who'd made the sneering suggestion. Linda the leader. They all looked up to her because she was pretty. Marijke stood behind the group. She didn't look at me. I should have ignored Linda and her smart remarks, but inside I bristled with fury and my blood boiled.

"Come on, Rikst. Let's go to class," Dirk suggested. He closed the door of my locker.

"Aren't you going to carry her books, Dirk?" Linda asked in her most sarcastic tone.

Marijke didn't say a word to me all morning. I was sorry. Every time I tried to make eye contact, she turned her head away. She ignored me totally, treating me as if I didn't exist.

Miss Oud rambled on about the short story contest and how the judges were busy reading the entries. One judge had informed her that it would be a hard decision this year because there were so many outstanding stories. On Wednesday there would be a special assembly in the gym to announce the winners. The two first prize winners would win a one-day trip to Amsterdam. Their stories would be entered in the National short story contest. I didn't really care about the contest anymore. All I wanted was a good mark and to find a solution to the mess I had worked myself into.

The day dragged on. At lunch time I sat with Bas and his friends. When I plunked down at their table, they looked puzzled. But I refused to sit with Marijke and her clique and listen to more insinuations. I felt alienated. A castaway like the other Rixt.

Finally the three-thirty bell rang. I walked out of the class ahead of everybody, grabbed my jacket from my locker and hurried to my bike.

Waiting outside was Thomas.

"Thomas. What's going on?"

"Can you and Bas come with me to the west end?"

"I can, but Bas has a dentist appointment."

"Do you have to let your Mom know?"

"No, she's working today. Can you tell me what's going on?"

"Yes, as soon as we're on our way."

I zipped up my jacket and jumped on my bike. I trailed behind Thomas out of the village. Once on the bike path, I came alongside. "What happened?"

"Do you think they've caught our three friends by now?"

I nodded.

"Well, they haven't."

"What!" I couldn't believe it. "Didn't we provide them with enough evidence?"

"One would think so."

"But have you seen the three smugglers today?" I asked.

We were pedaling at a good speed. Thomas might

be seventy, but he was in good shape. I could tell he was angry. His chin stuck forward, his mouth formed a thin line and his bushy, white eyebrows frowned.

"Not today. But last night I checked the ferry before it left. And wouldn't you know, the three of them were on the boat. Going back to the mainland. I didn't see any of the inspectors or Officer Kiewiet."

"But they could have been waiting for them on the mainland, couldn't they?"

"That's what I'd hoped," Thomas continued. "But just to check, I went back to the pier this morning and sure enough, they arrived back on the first boat."

My mouth fell open. "What's going on, I wonder. Or do you think they didn't believe us?"

"I don't know anymore, Rikst. But I was so angry and frustrated I just felt I needed to go for a bike ride, and I'd hoped you and Bas would accompany me," he mumbled in his mustache.

I smiled. Good old Thomas. He was a practical man. "Perhaps the police need to do some paperwork before they can arrest them."

"Oh, I wouldn't be surprised. Bureaucracy. Bureaucracy," he sighed. "Anyway, it's out of our hands now. You'd better show me the progress of the work on the dunes. That'll take my mind off all of this."

"Aye, captain. I'd love to."

We passed north of Hollum and rode to the lighthouse, where we left our bicycles at the gate. We headed down to the beach. The bulldozers were still piling sand against the dune that had been partially washed away during the storm. But now it was taking shape and the work was in its final stages. The dune was shaped like a cornucopia, with the slope of the point towards the sea.

"They're doing a great job," Thomas admired the work.

We walked for a while along the shoreline heading north. The waves, calm and patient today, rolled in even rhythm onto the beach. Seagulls dove into the waves to find their dinner. A sandpiper tripped ahead of us, his head bobbing up and down, his beak pecking in the sand in search of snails and worms. The tide was receding leaving behind transparent, blue jellyfish scattered on the beach. I picked up a starfish. My hand brushed the rough texture of its pointy body. I threw it back into the waves.

"Let's go back through the dunes," Thomas suggested.

The path led through a hollow. We were greeted by plovers and oyster catchers screeching low over our heads. They weren't used to seeing two-legged creatures this time of year. A pheasant flew ahead of us and a partridge hid in the underbrush as we tramped up the trails.

Dead leaves crunched beneath our boots. Thomas found a branch, straight enough to serve as a walking cane. I took a deep breath.

"I love this place," I said.

"Yes, so do I." Thomas turned to look at me. "You know what, Rikst? There aren't too many young people who love to be close to nature, who value solitude."

"I know. None of my friends do. They think I'm kind of crazy. They think I'm like Rixt, the witch."

Thomas shook his head.

"Thomas?"

"Yes."

"That night we found the body and I thought I'd seen the ghost of Rixt, you said you weren't surprised I'd seen her, but you never finished the sentence."

Thomas walked in silence. I turned to look at his face that was now one big frown.

"Thomas?" I asked softly.

"It was a stormy night. A bad one. You wouldn't remember. It must have been ten years ago." Thomas looked up. I could see he wasn't with me anymore. "I'd returned from the village," his voice sounded strained now. "Before I went home I climbed the dune to look at the sea. To hear the deafening sound of the breakers. To inhale that special smell. That's when I saw it."

"What, Thomas? Did you see her?"

"No. I saw the lights from a ship. A ship in trouble. Every now and then three flares went up." Thomas had slowed down. I looked at his face now twisted in pain.

"I just stood there, Rikst. I didn't do anything."

"What could you have done, Thomas. You were too far away from the boat. You were not near a phone."

"When I finally turned to go home, I saw her. The woman on top of the dune. Waving a lamp back and forth, back and forth. She wore a long cape and I saw her hair flying in the wind."

"Oh, Thomas. You think she had …" The words stuck in my throat.

"I looked at her and couldn't move. She must have been gone for a long time when my feet finally carried me back to the village. I went to the coast guard, but it was too late." Thomas paused. I knew without asking, this story didn't have a happy ending.

"The next day I found out that the ship in trouble had been the *Wilhelmina*. My good friend Barend was the captain. The sea took eight people that night, Rikst. Eight healthy, strong men. Fine men."

I looked into his grieving face and had no words to offer. My hand touched the sleeve of his duffel coat.

Without realizing it, our walk had taken us near the bunkers. "We better go back to the lighthouse," Thomas said.

"You want to see the grave we found?" I stopped and looked at the old skipper.

"No. We better not."

"It's close by. I'll show you. Maybe it isn't a grave. To Bas and me, it looked like a freshly dug grave."

"We've stayed away too long already. It will be dark

soon and your mom is probably home from work and wondering where you are."

"It's all right, Thomas," I pleaded. "It will only take a minute." I don't know why I found it so important that Thomas see the grave, but I felt a strong urge to show it to him. Maybe I still needed to convince him that there had been a dead body on the beach.

"Let's go then," he sighed.

"It's on the far side of the second bunker," I pointed the way.

We went through the hole in the fence that we'd seen the smugglers use. I never even considered that it might not be safe to go into the area. In spite of what Thomas had just told me, I felt that we'd seen the last of them. With the police on to them, surely they wouldn't be poking around here in broad daylight.

We made our way to the south side of the second bunker.

"What do you think, Thomas?" I said as we came close to the freshly dug up mound. "Is it a grave?"

"Yes, I think you're right," Thomas answered. "They probably buried the fourth man over here."

Then I heard something behind me. But before I could turn, an arm tightened around my throat and pulled me back. I screamed and kicked my legs. I saw Ice-woman walk up to me, her eyes cold as steel.

"Where is the little boy?" she yelled. "Is he still investigating the bunker?"

"No!" I cried. "He isn't with us."

She looked at me with doubt in her eyes.

Thomas lay on the ground. The Asian guy wrestled with him. I flung my arms back to fight my attacker. I only hit air. The Irishman held me with one arm. I kicked at his shin. This time my shoe found its mark. He let out a growl. After only a moment's hesitation I felt a short, sharp pain in my head and everything went dark.

.17.

"Aah!" It's dark in here. Why can't anybody turn on the light? I have to call someone. My voice … There's no sound.

I try to move. I'm stuck. I can't feel my arms. I've lost my arms. My head feels heavy. So heavy. It's stuck, too. Stuck to a cold surface. Concrete.

Concrete … The lighthouse. Thomas and I are tied together on the floor of the cellar of the lighthouse.

Ice-woman. She's coming back to kill me because I stole her name.

No. I stole Rixt's name. Mom gave me that name. Why?

"Thomas!" I pause.

"Thomas! Are you dead? Wake up! I have no arms!"

Tears run down my face. Oh, no! Thomas is dead and any minute they'll come back to kill me and throw me in the sea. My body starts shaking. What time is it? Is it morning? The middle of the night? I try to move. Only my legs move. Thomas and I are tied back to back in a sitting position and we've toppled over. That's why my head is on the concrete floor. My arms are trapped between our bodies and I can't feel them.

"Thomas! Answer, please! I don't want you to be dead. You are my friend."

My throat closes. I cough as if I'm being choked.

"Thomas! Help! Anybody! Piet! Help!"

Exhausted, I close my eyes.

I have to think. What to do next? Wait for the killers? Or scream for help for as long and as hard as I can?

"Huh?" Someone's at the door. Is it them?

"Help! We're in here! In the cellar!"

Voices …

Do they speak English?

NO.

Dutch?

There are many voices.

Dad's voice …

"Rikst! Thomas!"

Yes, it is Dad.

"Dad!" Or am I dreaming?

They're trying the door.

"Dad! Help! Thomas is dead!"

I writhe my body in agony. Please, let this be true. Let this be Dad.

Clang! The door bursts open. Lights poor in. Sharp beams of flashlights.

"Rikst. Oh, Rikst." Dad is beside me on the floor. He puts his arms around me. His wet face touches my cheek.

"Thomas is dead, Dad," I whisper.

"Sh," he says.

More voices surround me. I hear crying. Mom.

Someone cuts the rope that held us together. Next, the string around my wrists. I'm being lifted. Mom's arms encircle me. She presses her face against mine.

"Oh, Rikst. Oh, my baby. I thought I'd lost you, too."

Thomas is carried outside and placed on the ground.

"Yes, there's a pulse," a man's voice says. "He's coming around."

"Rikst, old girl, are you all right," Thomas' voice is hoarse.

"Yes," I answer, relieved. "I thought you were dead, Thomas." Tears fill my eyes.

"Put her down carefully. She probably has a concussion," another voice says.

It feels strange, but safe with Dad's arms around me.
My eyes close. My arms start to tingle. A prickling feeling travels slowly from my shoulders to the tips of my
fingers. But it doesn't matter. I'm not dead. Thomas isn't
dead. Because if he was, it would have been my f ...
Someone calls my name. Bas. I'm glad to hear his voice.

"Rikst! Oh, Rikst. I'm so glad you're safe." Marijke
throws her arms around me almost knocking my dad
off balance. He has to put me down.

"I'm sorry, Marijke, for not telling you," I hug her back.

"It's all right," Marijke smiles through her tears, "you
can tell me all the details later."

Another face comes into view. Dirk? What's he doing
here? My heart pounds wildly. He looks tired. There's
concern in his eyes. For an instant our eyes meet. A
smile lights up his face. A warm feeling envelops me.

Then, Mom's right beside me. She puts her arms
around me and gently pushes me in the direction of
our car. I see Thomas being moved to the police car.
Dad is now talking to Officer Kiewiet.

"We'll take you to the doctor first," Mom says, as she
closes the door on the passenger side.

Dad follows us inside the car and starts the engine.
"Officer Kiewiet and Thomas will meet us at the doctor's," he says. "We want to make sure neither of you
has any serious injuries."

•••

"No! Don't tie me up. Not again!"

"It's all right, Rikst. Nobody is tying you up. You are
safe. In your own bed. You had a nightmare, but other
than that you are fine. You just need some sleep to get
over the shock of last night's events."

Dad's voice soothes me. I look at him. I feel his hand
on my arm.

"Dad," I sigh. "Where is Thomas?"

"Thomas went home after the doctor checked him out and couldn't find anything wrong with him except for a nasty bump on his head. We offered to let him stay here for a few days, but you know Thomas."

I open my eyes. Dad sits on the edge of my bed and looks at me. He smiles. Deep creases are etched beside his mouth.

"I'm so glad he's not dead. It would have been my fault, Dad. I was scared, so scared."

"So were we, Rikst. We had no idea what the three of you were up to."

"No," I swallow. "We didn't realize what we'd gotten into and how dangerous these people were. Where are they? And how did you find us?"

"We got worried when you didn't show up for dinner. So we asked Bas."

"Bas didn't know," I murmur. "He was at the dentist."

"Yes," Dad nods. "He told us that you and Marijke had had a fight and maybe you were over at her place."

"No," I say. "You know I almost lost my best friend because of this. I was so glad to see her. But how did she get involved?"

"She is a true friend, Rikst. She was very concerned and helped us look for you."

"But Marijke didn't know where I was either."

"No. She suggested we ask Dirk."

"Dirk? Oh, yes. She's afraid Dirk and I have something going on because he has stopped teasing me."

"Anyway, Dirk said he'd seen you talking to Thomas."

"Yes, Thomas met me at the school to tell me that the police hadn't arrested the smugglers."

"When we didn't find you at Thomas' cottage, we went to the police. Bas told us about the drugs they'd hidden in the bunkers and shipped by fishing boat on Saturday night. Officer Kiewiet came with us to the bunkers. But there was no one. We even went inside. They were empty. He told us that five undercover officers would arrive with the eight o'clock ferry."

I yawn and my eyes close again.

"Get some sleep. I'll tell you the rest after."

"Are they locked up, Dad?"

"No, Rikst. They either smelled danger and got on the ferry as soon as they'd locked you up, or they were picked up by the fishing boat on the beach."

Dad's face brushes mine.

"I still don't know how you found us."

"Bas, Aunt Anna, Mom, Dirk, Marijke and I returned to the police station with Officer Kiewiet. There, we talked to the two inspectors you had met the day before. They told us that the three of you had tracked down a drug route from Taiwan to Ireland."

"Wow," I say. "So this was no small operation?"

"It certainly wasn't." Dad's face is serious. "The woman was the leader."

"Ice-woman," I say.

"The Asian guy was the contact person. He had connections in Taiwan. The Irishman was her accomplice. As soon as the five officers from the mainland arrived, they planned to surround the hotel and arrest the three suspects."

"That easy."

"Not exactly," Dad continues. "They weren't at the hotel. Although the brown station wagon was parked in the parking lot. We raced back to the bunkers. But there was no sign of them there either, or you and Thomas. By now we were convinced they had taken the two of you hostage." Dad looks away. "We never thought of the lighthouse though. We searched the conservation area and went over to the first bunker. If the smugglers had access to the second bunker they might have used the first one as well. Officer Kiewiet forced the lock off the barbed wired fence. We checked around the shelter in the bushes. We found nothing." Dad's voice quivers. "At last, we went inside." He shakes his head. "Defeated, we went back to the lighthouse. Officer Kiewiet went over to the guard's house and asked Piet if he had noticed any unusual activities. Then just as we were about to leave, Bas spotted the bicycles parked against the fence."

"The bikes were our only hope." I shiver under the covers. "Someone had to recognize them." Dad's hand brushes the hair away from my face.

"Piet and Officer Kiewiet went up the lighthouse, while we waited downstairs. My eyes were drawn to the door that said, KEEP OUT. It was a long shot but I wanted to open that door." Dad rubs his forehead.

When I remember the moment I heard voices outside the cellar, tears flood my eyes.

"We all listened and at the same time we heard a call for help."

So my desperate cries had not been in vain.

"When Piet and Officer Kiewiet came down to tell us that everything in the dome was normal, we asked him to open the door. That's when he noticed the key didn't fit the padlock. The lock had been changed. He cut the lock and you know the rest of the story."

"I'm so glad you found me. Me and Thomas." I sigh. "What time is it?"

"It's seven-thirty, so you'd better get some sleep," Dad rises from the bed and yawns. "I'll go to the office for a few hours. I'll be back at lunch time."

I hear the door close and drift into a restless sleep in which brown station wagons chase me through the dunes. All morning I slip in and out of the nightmare.

•••

"Are you awake?" Mom's head peeks around the door. Do you want to get up? Marijke called. She wants to visit you right after school."

"What time is it?" I look at my watch. It's close to three o'clock. "I can't believe it. I slept since Dad left this morning. Did you go to work?"

"Oh, no. When Dad came home at lunch we decided not to wake you. You must be hungry."

At that moment my stomach starts growling and we both laugh.

"I'll make you something to eat." Before she closes the door, Mom hugs me tight.

The spray of the shower feels good. It's like rinsing off the nightmare. I can think clearly again.

The aroma of pasta and sauce tickles my nose when I walk down the stairs.

"I think I can eat the whole pot, Mom," I say with my mouth full.

Mom sighs. She looks warily at me.

"I'm okay now, Mom."

Mom nods. She gets up and busies herself at the stove. "I made some for Thomas, too. Maybe Bas can take it to him after school."

"Can I go with him? I need to visit Thomas. Oh, Mom, I was so sure he was dead. I felt awful."

"You'd think a man of his age should know better than to get involved in something like this."

"But we didn't know it was so dangerous, Mom. Not until we found the drugs. And I should have never shown Thomas the grave. It was all my fault and if something had happened to him, I would have never forgiven myself." I put my fork down. All of a sudden I am not hungry anymore.

A knock at the door brings me back to life.

"Hi, Rikst. Hi, Aunt Nel. My mom's coming over later, she's making dessert for Thomas. I'm going to see him shortly and I wonder if you'd come with me, Rikst? Or are you not feeling up to it yet?"

"Can I, Mom?"

"Hello!" Marijke peeks around the corner.

"Oh, come in, Marijke."

"Does everybody want hot chocolate?" Mom straightens her face and walks over to the fridge.

Marijke takes off her coat, hugs me and puts a bouquet of flowers on my lap. "I'm sorry about the fight," she says.

"Me, too." I squeeze her arm. "Thanks for looking for me," I swallow, "and for the flowers."

Bas walks to the door. "I'll see if I can give my mom a hand. We'll be back." He turns around to face me. "I'm glad you're okay, Rikst. I'm sorry I wasn't there. Maybe the three of us could have fought them off."

"Not likely, Bas," I chuckle. "They were armed remember. But thanks anyway. I'm glad you were safely at the dentist."

"I'll see you," he smiles.

Marijke and I talk for a while and I let her in on all the details of our adventure.

"You are so daring," she says. "Will you be back at school, tomorrow? The girls won't tease you anymore. You have gained a lot of respect especially among the boys." Her eyes twinkle.

I feel my face turn hot. "Yes, I'll be there. I don't care what Linda and her gang say about me. The most important thing is that you're not mad at me anymore."

"Don't forget, tomorrow is the assembly for the story contest." Marijke zips up her coat and walks to the door. "See you. Thanks for the hot chocolate, Mrs. de Bruin."

The story contest had completely vanished from my mind. It seems a long time ago that I have written about Rixt and I really don't need to win. I'm happy to be home and alive. I look at Mom, who's filling a plastic container with pasta and sauce. She turns around and looks at me.

"Happy to be alive, Rikst? And I'm glad you're back with us." Mom smiles. Her face is pale with watery eyes.

.18.

"I don't think it's wise to go out now." Mom wipes her hands on her apron and looks at Aunt Anna. "We don't know if those people are off the island. They might be hiding somewhere. And you have a nasty bump on your head, Rikst."

Aunt Anna shakes her head. "I don't think they'd stick around. They might have left the island right after they locked up Rikst and Thomas, but I share your concern, Nel."

Bas looks at me. "It doesn't matter, Rikst. I'll take the food to Thomas and check up on him."

"If we could just convince that stubborn old skipper to buy a phone." Mom sighs and looks at me. She doesn't want me to go, I can tell. I don't really want to go either. My head does hurt, but I won't let Mom know that. My worst fear is that Ice-woman and her crew might still be around. I won't feel safe until they're behind bars. But I don't want to let Bas down and I want to check on Thomas, as well.

"No, I'll come with you. It's still early and I'm sure those smugglers don't want to be seen even if they are on the island." I say it more bravely than I feel at this moment.

"Please be careful," Mom hugs me. "Tonight we have to talk, you and I."

"It's okay, Mom. It can wait. You have to be sure

you're ready to tell me." With the back of my hand, I touch her cheek.

"I am ready," she whispers, before I close the door behind me and follow Bas to the shed.

We place the containers with food in my saddle bags and pedal off into the dusk.

Our long shadows follow us where the streetlights illuminate the road. My eyes dart from buildings to parked cars and I'm constantly looking over my shoulder.

Darkness engulfs us by the time we reach Sand Dike. I shiver in my coat.

"Stop, Bas!" Panic paralyzes my limbs. "Let's follow the trail through the dunes again. I'm terrified."

"Are you afraid they're still around?" Bas drags his bike over the first dune and I stumble right behind him. My eyes are adjusting to the dark and the white sand shows us the way.

"Yes," I startle myself with that answer. "I can feel them. They are here. This is my imagination working overtime. You can laugh at me."

"No, I won't laugh at you." Bas pulls up right beside me. His hand touches my arm. "You should have stayed home, Rikst. Do you want to go back?"

"No, we need to check on Thomas." I feel shaky and sweat's pouring down my forehead.

When we reach the cottage it is cloaked in darkness.

"Perhaps he's in bed. Don't worry yet, Rikst." Bas walks to the front door and rings the bell. We wait but Thomas doesn't answer.

"You think he's out?" Bas asks.

"No. Something is wrong." My legs feel unsteady and I lean against the door.

"Wait here. I'll go around to the back door."

I don't want Bas to leave me. My feet stay rooted to the spot.

"Rikst! Come here!" His scream startles me and alarm bells ring in my head. In a trance, I move to the back of the cottage. Bas points at a small window beside the door. Glass splinters are scattered all over the interlocking stones.

I have no words. Fear tightens my throat and settles into my stomach. Bas reaches for the door handle. It opens.

"Thomas!" he calls and turns on the light. We walk through the laundry room into the kitchen. Bas flicks on the second light switch.

I gasp when I see the body lying on the floor in a dark puddle of blood. In an instant, I'm on my knees beside Thomas on the floor.

"Quick, Bas. Go back into town. At the first house phone an ambulance, the police and our parents. Don't look at me. Go!"

Bas gapes at me. "But Rikst, they might come back!"

"I don't care. Go! I'll stay with him." My arms wave hysterically at Bas, motioning him to leave.

Without a word Bas leaves the cottage. Now I have a chance to look at my friend. Now he *is* dead. What I'd feared last night has come true today. I fight down the nausea that swirls in my stomach.

Thomas' body is stretched out on the floor. His head is turned to the side. The blood is on the side facing me. I take one arm, place my fingers on his wrist and try to feel for a pulse. But I'm so shaky I can't feel a thing.

"Thomas," I whisper. "Thomas." Warm tears stream down my face and drip on Thomas' hand.

"Please, don't be dead. Please, Thomas." I stay on my knees and hold his hand. It feels cold. "Oh, Thomas. Do you remember how you used to make the most magnificent sand castles on the beach? And one time we built a pirate ship out of sand. You told us you'd fought one of these pirate ships and scared them away."

I pause and look at his lifeless face. "I believed that story for the longest time." Where the skin isn't covered in blood, the coloring is gray white. The tiny blood veins seem to lay on top of the skin like purple lines drawn by a fine marker.

Slowly I get up. I grab a towel from the cupboard underneath the sink and soak it under the tap. I'm not really sure why I'm doing this, but I begin to clean his head. Gently, I place the wet towel on his face. The blood is mostly dry, so he must have been lying here for a while. My heart is pounding in my ears. The smugglers will come back. The feeling of Ice-woman breathing cold fire down my neck, makes me shiver.

Focusing on my task, I wash most of the blood from Thomas' hair and his face. Afterwards, I clean the blood off the vinyl floor. Thomas's clean face is still a pale gray. Then, I remember, dead people are supposed to feel cold and stiff.

Trembling fingers touch the skin of his neck. It's still warm. Perhaps he just died and isn't cold yet. Where's Bas? What's taking him so long? My eyes fly around the room, taking everything in at once. All my senses are on high alert. Did I hear a noise?

"Rikst?"

With a jolt I sit up. "Thomas. You are alive?" I can't believe it when my old friend slowly opens his eyes.

"Oh, Thomas." Choking, I grab his hand.

Thomas closes his eyes again. He moves his head and groans.

"What did they do to you?"

With effort, Thomas speaks. "Wa–ter."

I let go of his hand and get up to find a cup and fill it with water. In the cupboard I see a box with straws, which Thomas keeps for us. The water spills on the floor when I try to help him drink the liquid through the straw.

"They were hiding in the cottage." He stops. "Last

night, when I came home."

Thomas' hand searches for mine and I place my warm trembling hand in his cold one.

"They're here, Rikst." His breathing comes in long and short gasps. "You should go to the police. Tonight they will be picked up. On the beach."

I give him time to speak. I can see Thomas is in pain.

"The same place. Do you remember how to get there, Rikst?" He closes his eyes. I listen to the silence of the cottage and Thomas' ragged breathing.

"You have to show the police the place, Rikst."

I nod. I can't speak. My body and mind are frozen in terror. At any moment the door will open and Ice-woman with her hateful eyes will come in and kill us both. I don't want to go out in the dunes and find them. I'm too scared.

"You will show them, won't you?" Thomas is reading my mind.

I nod again. Thomas closes his eyes. He murmurs something but I can't understand him.

A sound at the back door. My blood stirs. Is it them? Or Bas?

The door opens. I'm afraid to look.

"Rikst. They're coming." Bas walks into the kitchen, swallowing his breath in big gulps.

"He's not dead, Bas." I move over so Bas can kneel beside Thomas.

"I'm so glad he's not dead." My voice quivers. "But they're still here. Thomas said they'll be picked up tonight."

While he catches his breath, Bas looks at me with eyes wide in disbelief. "I can't believe they didn't get off the island." He wipes his forehead with the sleeve of his jacket. His eyes turn to Thomas. "He's in bad shape."

My eyes fill up. I don't bother to wipe my face. I let the tears drip on my hands.

We both love this man. He's our friend. When I look at Bas, his eyes glisten too.

Then there is a commotion at the door. Loud voices. Terrified we look up. It can't be them. It is help we've been waiting for.

"Rikst! Bas!" Officer Kiewiet's voice sounds through the laundry room. The door opens and he fills the kitchen.

"They've beaten him so badly." It finally hits me hard and my body shudders with sobs.

"Sh. Wait. Let's wait for the doctor to check him first." Officer Kiewiet pats my back. "Let's give them some room." When Doctor de Vries and two other men with a stretcher enter the kitchen, Bas and I move to the window.

Bas stands to the side. His white face staring at Thomas.

"Well, we have a pulse," Doctor de Vries looks at me. I slowly let out my breath.

"Our parents are coming," Bas says in a soft voice. "As soon as your mom can get a hold of your dad, they'll get my mother and come over."

I look outside, but can't see a thing. I hope they'll be here soon. At this moment I want to be with my parents very much.

Doctor de Vries places his stethoscope on Thomas' chest. "And the skipper's old heart is still beating, Rikst. It takes more than a few drug smugglers to finish off this man. Take him." He motions to the two men with the stretcher. "I don't want to take any risks and examine him in my office. He could have internal injuries. We'll move him as little as possible and fly him to the mainland right away."

We follow the procession out of the cottage. They carry Thomas over the dune, where the ambulance is waiting on the road.

All of a sudden we are surrounded by men. Men in dark clothes. I recognize the two detectives who were at the police station Sunday morning. But I have no idea who the other people are.

One of the men comes up to me. He's tall with short, dark hair and a mustache.

"You must be Rikst," he says in a friendly voice. "My name is Smid. We realize that you are very upset." My eyes are drawn to the revolver in the holster on his belt.

"I'm afraid that we may need your help to find the people who did this to your friend. But you know how dangerous they are." He looks at me intently. "They are still on the island, aren't they?"

"Yes. And tonight they will be taken off the island by the same fishing boat that came to pick up the drugs last Saturday. Thomas just told me." The words come out in a rush.

"Do you know where they meet these friends with the fishing boat?"

My head nods like a robot.

"You think you can lead us to the place where they make contact?"

Again I nod. I fail to speak. The words are stuck. Trapped. The whole nightmare is starting all over.

"I'll be with you," Bas takes my hand. "We'll show you where the place is, Officer."

I pull my hand back. "Where's my dad?" I look at Bas. "I want him to come with me."

Bas moves his right foot back and forth in the sand. "Any time," he says. "He'll be here."

"Which way, Rikst?" Officer Kiewiet seems to be in charge now. "You and Bas go ahead and we'll follow. We won't use our flashlights. So it will be dark." My eyes follow his as he looks up into a threatening, dark sky. "The moon is not going to assist us tonight," he sighs and looks at us.

I hesitate. I want to wait for my parents.

"We have to go now," Officer Kiewiet urges. "We don't want them to escape."

.19.

With reluctance, I climb the first dune. Bas is right behind me. I don't know where the others are. I don't
care. I'm walking in a cold night. In a bad dream. I
hope I wake up in my own warm bed. Forcing myself,
moving one foot ahead of the other, I stumble over
clumps of grass, trip over branches, scratch my hands
and face on the thorns of bushes.

Black forms and dark hollows make me skittish. I
want to go back.

Bas helps me get up when I fall and bang my knee
on a piece of driftwood. Up one dune and down another. No one talks. I can't hear the men behind me.
Or did we lose them already?

"Wait." I grab onto Bas' sleeve.

"They're right behind us," Bas urges me on. "We'll
go down to the last row of dunes," he says. "From there
we move east."

I don't speak. I'm glad Bas's taking over. I don't want
to make any decisions right now. I'm tired and terrified. From the moment we entered Sand Dike, I've felt
the presence of Ice-woman. I have the feeling she's
watching me in this dark, moonless night. A bird of
prey, ready to fall from the sky with her magnificent
claws to tear me apart. This time there will be no rescue.

"There, Rikst." Bas catches up with me. "There's the
North Sea."

I look up. We've reached the top of the last row of dunes. I hear the waves hitting the beach. A comforting sound. For an instant I let the sound and the smell envelop me. The wind is moderate tonight blowing from the northwest. The cold air feels good on my hot face.

"Stay down," Bas tugs at my arm. I see that with his other arm he signals to the men below us.

When he reaches us, Officer Kiewiet is huffing and puffing like an old steam engine. The other officers and detectives follow right behind him. They seem to be in much better shape than our man of the law. It's ironic that a man like him has been given the responsibility of a whole island. I'd never thought about it before.

They all gather around when Officer Smid starts to talk. His voice is deep and calm. "We'll move east until we find out which dune they use to signal their accomplices." He looks around the circle, but I don't think he can read any of the faces; it is too dark. From a distance I hear the rumbling of the waves. I feel an urge to go down to the water and let the sounds take over my senses.

"Once we find out which dune they're on, we'll spread out and encircle them on the beach," Officer Smid continues. His face turns towards the sea. "Our only problem is the beach. The distance from the dunes to the water line is about three hundred meters. Is that about right, Officer Kiewiet?"

"Yes, that's correct," Officer Kiewiet answers.

"That means three hundred meters out in the open. We can't wait until they're in the boat. That'll be too late. We'll have to go down low, so by the time they're ready to jump into the dinghy, we pounce on them." He pauses. "Everybody got that?"

The men around us mumble. I don't know what to say and I have no idea what is expected from me. There's no way I'm going to pounce on Ice-woman and her gang.

"We have to use the element of surprise as much as we can," Officer Smid continues. "Once we're down on the beach, we'll have to crawl on our stomachs and try to get as close as possible to the dinghy before we're spotted. Rikst and Bas?" I am startled when he addresses us. "How many people came in the dinghy last Saturday night?"

"Two," Bas and I answer in unison.

"That's five altogether and we are eight. We should be able to get the better of them."

Eight, he said. That leaves Bas and me out. I wonder what he has in mind for us to do?

"How many more dunes to the east, kids?"

"Four or five," Bas answers.

"Let's move, people."

Our small procession continues to move slowly eastward with Bas and me still in the lead. We stay low so as not to be seen from the beach. I think that it is quite unlikely that we could be seen anyway; in the darkness I can barely see my own feet.

Then my foot gets caught in a clump of marram grass and I tumble head first down the side of a dune. When I finally come to rest at the bottom, I grab my head and close my eyes. My temples throb and there is a pain above my right eye.

"Are you hurt?" Bas kneels beside me at the bottom of the dune.

"No, I'm all right." I scramble to my feet and with Bas' support head out to the next dune. Tonight they feel like mountains instead of sand hills.

We gather together near the top of the fifth dune. Officer Smid defines the plan of action. "We wait till we see their signals," he says. "Then you two," he points at two plain-clothes detectives, "work yourselves around these dunes to the east of where the smugglers are.

Jansma, Kiewiet and Hiddinga, you climb on the south side of the dune and follow the suspects from behind. Boorsma, Dekker and myself will close in from this end. Rikst and Bas, I want you to stay in this spot. Make sure you're invisible and don't move. Stay as low as possible just in case we have to use our weapons."

This is fine with me. I don't want any part of the action. Last night had been enough adventure for me for a long while. I can feel Bas' disappointment, but he keeps silent. These men with their stern faces are more intimidating than Officer Kiewiet.

We all settle down to wait. My eyes scan the North Sea. I don't see any lights from boats. What if they've decided to meet their friends at another part of the island. We could be out here all night.

Lying on my stomach, I rest my head on my arms. As soon as I close my eyes, I see Ice-woman. Her cold eyes glare at me. Her voice a raspy sound.

"Rikst." Bas nudges my shoulder. "Look straight ahead. See those three lights."

I lift up my head and strain my eyes in the direction Bas points. Then, I see them. "The lights are similar," I say.

"Officer Smid," Bas' voice sounds low. "The lights in the distance, straight ahead, could be the boat."

"Thanks, Bas." The officer rises on his knees. "It's still too far from the shore. We wait till it moves closer or we see their signal."

The next minutes feel like hours. Bas moves restlessly beside me. I watch the lights come nearer. Far in the distance the lights of another ship slowly crawl east. The three small lights come closer. It must be the pick-up boat. My heart starts pounding. The three smugglers are near. Ice-woman is probably standing on the next dune. So close I can feel her. My eyes search the outline of the dune beside us.

"Yes!" I gasp when the first flash lights the dark night. In response, a light moves back and forth on the next dune, outlining the ghostly figure with long hair. The men beside us move quickly and by the time the second flash casts its light, they're gone. Bas and I are left alone. The swinging light brings my thoughts back to Rixt. This is how she must have stood on top of the dune, waving her light, tricking trusting sea captains and endangering the lives of innocent seamen. Just like the story of the *Wilhelmina*.

"Bas," I whisper. I roll over expecting to find Bas beside me. He's gone. On my knees, I crawl up the dune. No Bas. Where did he go? Did he follow the men after all without telling me?

"Bas!" I call a little louder. Panic surrounds me like a wall. "Bas!" I call out again. Without thinking, I stumble down the other side of the dune. I see a dark shape running down the dune in my direction. It must be Bas, I think. "Bas!" I call again. I've forgotten to be quiet and invisible. "Bas!" I run towards the shadow that moves towards me. "Why did you leave me alone?"

As the form comes nearer, I begin to focus more clearly on what is happening. This isn't Bas! My heart stops. My feet freeze to the sand. Then the wind betrays my opponent, blowing her long hair to one side. I want only to disappear into the dune. If the sand would just open and swallow me.

For one moment we stand face-to-face. In the next second she throws herself on top of me. Together we crash onto the sand. I try to roll but she grabs me from behind. Her claws dig in my arms and she pulls me upright. One arm clamps around my neck and a hard object pokes me in the small of my back.

"You miserable little witch." She grinds her teeth and prods me ahead of her. "I can't make a move without you being in my way. You don't give up, do you?"

I feel her breath on my neck. It sends icicles down my spine. I stumble along. She pushes me over the last dune.

"This time you will not escape. I'm taking you with me."

My brain starts to work again. She's taking me … as a hostage! Oh, no. She's taking me on the dinghy. And once at sea … I close my eyes. We stumble. She pulls me up and drags me along. This woman is strong. Nausea fills my stomach. Ice-woman breathes cold fire down my neck.

I have to do something. Suddenly I feel a surge of energy, a rush of adrenaline, I guess. Lying in the dunes with Bas and the police detectives had terrified and drained me completely. I had lost all aspiration for adventure. I had been terrified simply by the *thought* of Ice-woman. But now, confronted with her in the flesh — and knowing that she intends to toss me into the North Sea as soon as I am of no more use to her — I feel a wave of energy that feeds on the fear and anger that envelops me.

"Down!" she yells in my ear. At the same moment she crushes my body with her own. We are close to the beach, my face half-buried in the sand. I wriggle my head and turn it towards Ice-woman. My heart's in my throat. She stares at me with cold, hateful eyes.

"The body," I say, speaking in English. "Did you take the body?"

"Nosy." Her voice rasps. I've never met a person with such a terrible voice.

"Because we have to stay put for a little while and you won't have a chance to tell my story, we might as well entertain each other." Her chuckle sounds like a squeaky wheelbarrow.

"We were four people first," she says. "But you didn't know us then. Pete, the man whose body you found on the beach, tried to break his contract with me. I'm the boss of this operation, you see and no one plays games with me. Especially not a stupid little girl like you." Her claws pinch my arm. The pain pierces through my winter jacket. My jaws clamp together. I won't give her the satisfaction of seeing that she's hurt me.

"What happened to him?" I don't know why I have the nerve to ask her.

"Once on board the trawler, he got into a fight with the captain. He *fell* overboard. The next day he washed ashore and you found him before we did." Her eyes scan the beach.

"Now, it's time to go," she says urgently. She pulls me up. Her vice-like arm reaches around my neck and pulls me against her body. I cough.

"And Rixt? Why did you dress and act like her?" I have to ask this question.

"Because you island people are stupid and superstitious. Now, shut up and run!" She pushes me forward. Her knees bump the back of my legs. Once in the open I can see the dinghy close to shore. It's small light bobbing up and down with the surf.

Where is everybody? I turn my head. I want to look back. I stumble over my own legs but she manages to keep me upright, her arm almost choking me.

"Keep your head straight and run!" I can now hear fear in her voice. We run. No. She runs. My feet can't find the pattern. Even though she's not much taller than me, she drags me through the sand. Sometimes my heels dig in the sand, making deep ruts; then, my legs cross over each other and I dance a foreign jive. In the middle of the beach, she stops. She turns me around and we face the dunes. I scan the sand. By now the men must be crawling towards the water. Nothing moves. Oh, my God. Have they changed their minds? Maybe Officer Smid decided the operation was too dangerous. The open beach wouldn't give them any protec … My heart leaps. There. On the east side. Small mounds are moving in our direction. Ice-woman must have noticed them, too. Her body jolts. Her arm tightens.

"I have the girl!" her voice booms. The wind blowing from the sea carries her words to the men on the beach.

"I have the girl!" she repeats. "I'll shoot her if you come close!"

Where are her two friends I wonder? Did they already capture the big Irish guy and the little Asian?

The small mounds have stopped moving. No one responds to Ice-woman's call. They can't do anything. Ice-woman calls the shots because she holds me hostage. Will they try? My hope dwindles. If they try, she'll kill me right here on the beach. I will be another dead body in the sand. Or will she throw me in the cold waves and I'll wash ashore with the tide? No! I don't want to die! I move my arms and try to turn my head.

"Hold still! You stupid idiot!"

She turns me around and we face the sea. "Move!" She pushes the revolver into my back. It hurts. But the pain is not important. My life is. As the waves roll in to meet us, my chances of escape diminish. The dinghy is pulled up on the sand. Two men stand beside it.

Ice-woman stops for the second time and spins me around. Again, I scan the beach.

"I have the girl!" her voice cries out. From the corner of my eye I see commotion at the dinghy. I hear a splash. The engine splutters. Are the guys coming to get us? My heart pounds so loud it hurts in my chest.

"I'll tell you about your stupid legend when we're out at sea," she hisses in my ear. She drags me over to where I hear the dinghy. Any moment I expect hands to grab me and pull me on board.

"*Kreee*!" A seagull-like cry rips from Ice-woman's

throat. Her arm suffocates me. This is it. The end. For the second time in twenty-four hours I have a near death experience, except this time it really happens.

Gasping for air, I see dead bodies on the beach. More bodies. From all sides now. The bodies are moving. Why isn't she killing me? The bodies are coming closer.

I tense all over. Any time now I'll hear the explosive sound of her gun; then, it will be all over.

"*Waah*," a dark monster throws us to the ground. This must be death. I haven't heard the shot. I must have missed it. Everything turns black.

.20.

Voices. The weight leaves my body. The vice is gone from my neck. Air fills my lungs in uneven gulps.

"Rikst!"

They must know me here, wherever I am.

I'm dead.

"Rikst!" I hear more clearly now. It is Bas' voice!

"Bas!" With a jolt, I sit up. Sand sprays into my mouth and nose. I cough and choke. An arm supports me. I'm not dead.

"Where's Ice-woman?" My voice sounds hoarse. My throat hurts.

"We got her." Officer Smid kneels beside me. His arm supports me.

"Take her up, men. I'll look after our little heroine." He calls his orders in a steady voice.

"Heroine? I was scared like a snared hare."

"You can say that," he laughs and helps me onto my feet. "Can you walk?"

I nod. "My neck and my throat hurt." Then I notice Bas. He walks beside us. His head down.

"Where were you, Bas? You left me alone. Then, she grabbed me."

"I'm sorry, Rikst. I should have told you. It looked like you were sleeping and I thought we were in a safe spot. I just had to …" He pauses. "I went down the side of the dune in the bushes. When I came back, you were gone." He sighs.

"Even if you had been there, what could you have done, Bas? The woman carried a weapon. What about the men in the dinghy?" My brain is slowly placing the events in order.

"As they landed, they realized what was going on and took off." Officer Smid keeps his arm around my shoulders as we walk towards the dunes.

"They won't get that far," he continues. "The coast guard has been warned and they will pick them up at sea."

"Where are the two other smugglers?"

"They walked right into our detectives' arms. We took them completely by surprise. But the woman wasn't with them. And unfortunately, she ran into you."

"Yes, she stumbled upon me, I guess. Or maybe she saw us when she was on top of the dune. I was in her way again, she said. But this time I was not going to escape."

We make the rest of our trek back to Thomas' cottage in silence. It takes forever. I stumble and trip. The night is still dark, but at least the fear is gone. Now I feel only tired and shaky.

After climbing over the last dune, we see the lights from Thomas' cottage. Bas runs ahead. I have no power left to run.

"Rikst! Rikst!" Mom and Dad's voices sound like music. I break free from the Officer and throw myself at my parents.

"Oh, Rikst," Mom cries. Dad's arms encircle us both. Aunt Anna and Bas join our circle. No one speaks. I look around the circle of faces. Love-filled eyes return my gaze. A slow warmth spreads from my heart, through my whole body and takes away the numb feeling that had come over me.

"How's Thomas?" I ask.

"We'll call the hospital as soon as we get home," Dad answers.

•••

"Good morning, Rikst. How are you feeling?" Mom opens the curtains and the room brightens.

"What time is it?"

"Eleven. You must have dozed off again since I last checked on you."

"How's Thomas?"

"He has internal injuries, broken ribs, a punctured lung and a bad concussion. I'll call again at lunch time. But thank goodness, he's still alive." Mom wipes tears from her face and sits down on the bed. Her hand trembles as she brushes hair away from my cheeks.

"I'm okay, Mom." I stroke her arm.

We stay like this. Mom and me.

"Would you like something to drink?" She looks at me.

"Something cold, please, my throat feels like sandpaper."

Mom leaves the room and I snuggle back under the cover. I shiver again, pinching myself, feeling that I'm not dead, but in my warm bed in my cozy room. Safe.

"Do you remember that today is the day they announce the winners of the contest?" Mom walks in with a tray. She hands me a glass with a white, foamy drink.

"Mmm, milkshake." I sip from the straw until I feel the ice cold liquid soothe my throat.

"It must be Wednesday," I sigh. "I really don't care if I win, Mom."

"I know." She bustles around my room with a duster. "You wrote a good story. And we shall talk. You and I. About your name."

"It's okay, Mom. If you're not ready, I can wait. It's not important anymore. I like my name."

"No. I want to tell you. But first I have to make lunch.

Dad's coming home today."

"It's all right, Mom. You can tell me some other time."

Funny, before this all happened I was determined to find out about my name. Now I am just happy to be alive.

Dad eats his lunch in my room and tells me about work. He looks tired.

"The island is buzzing with rumors," he says. "Rumors, how you and Bas and Thomas broke a drug smuggling operation."

"As if we set out to do that, Dad. Like always, people exaggerate."

Dad nods. "Well, I'm off to work."

After lunch Mom comes to tuck me in. "Have a nap," she says. "After, we'll talk."

Mom's still putting it off. I feel sorry for her. She seems nervous. I regret having bugged her so much about my name.

•••

Voices wake me. I hear footsteps on the stairs.

"You have visitors." Mom opens the door.

Marijke peeks from behind my mother.

"Hi," she says. "I brought someone with me. I hope you don't mind?"

A movement behind her catches my eye. Dirk. Dirk's here to visit me?

Marijke moves aside. "Dirk wants to know how you are and he has something important to tell you."

Surprised, I look from Marijke to Dirk. What can be important?

"Hi," Dirk says. I feel the blood rushing to my face. I don't know what to say. Dirk's eyes are serious. He doesn't act arrogant.

"I brought you something," he says. He walks over

to my bed and places a rectangular wrapped box on the cover. I'm afraid to look at him. My bedroom seems awfully small now that Dirk fills the room.

My fingers tremble when I carefully take off the paper. Inside is a box. The cover tells me the box is filled with expensive chocolates. I don't know what to say.

Embarrassed, I look up. His eyes meet mine and they smile.

"Remember the contest?" He breaks the awkward silence.

I nod.

"Today we had an assembly in the gym and the mayor announced the two winners." He pauses. "You have won the second prize."

"Oh!" I can't believe it.

"Congratulations, Rikst."

"Thanks, Dirk. And, oh, thanks for helping in the search party." I stumble over my own words. My eyes fill up. I look away. Yuk. My stupid tears fall freely these last few days. And I hate crying in front of others. "Thanks, Dirk. For the chocolate."

"I better leave. I'm sure you and Marijke have lots to catch up on." He stands at the door and looks at me, his eyes dark and sincere.

"Wait, Dirk. Who won first prize?"

"Me," he says and closes the door behind him.

Stunned, I look at Marijke.

"Isn't it wonderful," she claps her hands. "You and Dirk will go to Amsterdam together."

I hadn't even thought of that. It takes a few seconds for Marijke's words to sink in.

"Aren't you jealous?"

"Yes. No. Of course, I wish it had been me. Just like all the other girls in our class."

I feel embarrassed. And confused.

Another knock at the door.

"You have more visitors. I better go. Will you be back at school tomorrow?"

"Yes," I nod.

Bas opens the door. "Hi, you're having a busy afternoon."

What are you holding behind your back?"

"Something I worked long, hard hours on. And it's for you." He steps forward and hands me a long, brown package. I unwrap the paper.

"Oh, Bas." My voice is wedged in my throat. Amazed, I stare at the wooden statue in my hands.

"You never liked the witch in Buren," he smiles.

"It's Rixt! Oh Bas, you made her out of that large piece of driftwood. She's beautiful." My cheeks feel wet. I don't care. Bas has seen me cry before.

"You think she's okay?"

"Okay?" I laugh. "She's perfect. She's the Rixt from my story."

"Yes, she's the Rixt from your story." Bas looks pleased.

Mom stands beside me. "I don't know how you do it, Bas. Look at her hair, Rikst.

It looks like you carved each hair separately. Even the folds in her cape and the way she stares out into the distance, waiting for her son to return." Mom's eyes mist. She strokes the wood. Her hand trembles.

"Congratulations on your prize." Bas laughs.

"Too bad you didn't win. Yours was good, too."

"I never expected to win. You want to be a writer. So this is a good start."

"Who told you I want to be a writer?" I had never told anybody except my paper friend.

"I know you like a sister, Rikst," Bas laughs.

"Thanks, brother," I smile.

We talk about the smugglers. "I'll tape it for you if it's on the news," he says before he leaves.

"Thanks. See you."

Just before supper I take a shower and get dressed. The house is filled with flowers from friends and relatives. Boukje phones and I talk to her for a while. She's surprised to hear that the three strange tourists had more up their sleeves than kissing on the ferry.

We all wait for the eight o'clock news on television. The island is in the news and the announcer tells the story of the drug smugglers. Most of it washes over me. I'm too tired. When they show the bunkers, I become alert. The camera zooms in on the grave which is now empty.

"The body of a fourth man has been found in a grave beside one of the bunkers," the newscaster reads. "According to the police, he's also from Ireland. He apparently tried to escape back to Ireland on the fishing vessel. After a scuffle on the deck of the boat, the man fell overboard. His body washed ashore the next day. Two young students discovered the dead man on the beach. But when they went for help and returned to the same spot, the body had vanished. It is believed that the woman and her two accomplices spirited their man away as soon as the students left and later buried him beside the bunker. It is not yet known how much heroin has been smuggled from Asia to Ireland via this route, but police estimate value to be in the hundreds of thousands of guilders at the very least. In other news … "

"So you were right about the body, Rikst," Dad says. "And you were right about Ice-woman being the ghost of Rixt."

"Yes, especially after she'd visited Mom at the museum and let on that she knew more about the legend than Mom expected."

Dad phones the hospital to find out how Thomas is.

"He's still in intensive care, but the nurse said he's stubborn enough to pull through. We can visit on the weekend."

I feel a bit relieved, but I'm anxious to see for myself that he's going to be all right. Tiredness takes over and I go back to my room. I need to share my feelings with my paper friend.

"I'll come and say goodnight," Mom says.

Dad looks at me and winks. I nod. He knows.

●●●

It's quiet in the house. I lay on my back on my bed. My diary held in my hands. The pen is on my night table. I try not to think about my experiences, but the fear is still there draped like a cloak around my body. I shift my thoughts to Mom, who at this moment is building up courage to tell me the story of my name. From downstairs, I can hear my parents' murmuring voices.

Now I'm waiting for Mom. She will tell me her secret tonight. I look at the statue on my dresser and smile. This one looks better. This Rixt stands up straight. She is much younger than the old hag in Buren. Her cape billows in the wind. Her long, straight hair blows to one side. In her right hand she carries a light, held high. Her expression is proud. Her eyes look distant. Bas has done an excellent job. Some day, he will be a renowned artist.

I hear footsteps on the stairs. Mom.

She stops in front of my door. I hear her walk into her own bedroom. The footsteps return. The door opens. Mom walks in. She carries the music box. I'm not surprised.

"Aren't you going to ask me why I brought this?" she pulls one of the rattan chairs up beside my bed and sits down.

"No, Mom. It's your turn to talk." I watch how she strokes the swans gently.

"It's not easy and I don't know how to start." She shifts in the chair.

"I know." I pat her knee.

"I was sixteen and in my last year of high school when I discovered I was pregnant." Crimson flushes her face. I don't say anything. She looks at me. Then, looks away. "I know what you're thinking. There was protection in those days, too."

"Don't, Mom. Don't do that." I feel hot. My palms are damp. The baby in the picture. Where is it? Did she give it up for adoption?

"When I was sixteen, being pregnant was still the worst thing that could happen to a girl. Nowadays young people have to worry about much more than pregnancy. There are so many terrible diseases out there. And getting pregnant doesn't seem the end of the world anymore."

I nod to encourage her to go on.

"Of course, here on the island, people were, and still are, very conservative in those matters. I knew my parents would be very upset."

I could hardly imagine my kind grandparents in that role.

"My mother cried that I had scandalized the whole family, put them to shame. My father yelled and threatened to kick me out of the house."

"Grandfather? Grandfather said that?" I find that hard to believe.

"They finally decided that it would stay a big secret. Only the three of us would know. They sent me away to a great-aunt in Amsterdam. An aunt I hardly knew."

"What about the father of the baby?" I ask. "Did he not have the right to know?"

"Not according to my father. The boy who had done this to his daughter could only be a jerk. And he forbid me to see him again. Not even to say good-bye."

"Oh, Mom." I try to imagine how heartbroken Mom must have been. I can't.

Mom looks down at the swans. A lock of brown curls conceals her eyes. She wets her lips.

"My parents told everybody in town that I would finish high school in Amsterdam and stay with the aunt, who had become seriously ill. She couldn't be alone.

It was hard living in Amsterdam. The aunt lived downtown, in a small apartment. I hated the noise. The traffic. People everywhere. It was never quiet. I missed the sea, the beach and the walks through the dunes."

Mom looks at the wall, her eyes are turned inward to the time when she was so young and lived through so much hardship.

"School was okay, at first. But when my body changed and I could no longer conceal my pregnancy, the teasing began. The girls were mean. I quit school and helped my aunt, who was arthritic. In time we got used to each other, but we were never close. My parents visited me only once during that time before the baby was born.

One night the pains came, though it wasn't time yet. With the help of a midwife, the baby was born. She was four weeks early."

I swallow. The baby in the picture.

"She was so pretty, Rikst. With her black hair sticking all over. Her dark eyes, so alert. I named her Rixt. After the woman in the legend. I'd always been intrigued by the story. So often I had imagined what it must have been like to be a castaway. To fend for yourself. And during my time away from the island I felt like an outcast. I often thought about Rixt."

"Mom."

She doesn't hear me. Her eyes are glistening.

"During the next few days my baby's health deteriorated. My parents came and took her to the hospital. The doctors found something wrong with her heart. She needed an operation."

Mom stops speaking. She wipes her eyes with the

back of her hand.

"The night before she was scheduled to have surgery, she died in my arms."

"Oh, Mom," I reach for her.

Mom takes my hand. She cries soundlessly. My eyes fill.

"She was so precious, Rikst. So sweet and tiny. So helpless."

I nod and swallow.

"After the funeral I didn't go home with my parents. I couldn't go back. I stayed another year in Amsterdam to finish high school."

"And the father?" I asked softly. "Did he ever find out about his little baby girl?"

"No." Mom shakes her head.

I think about Dirk's words about his father and Mom. Was Dirk's father the father of the baby? I watch Mom's face. It's closed. She will never tell me that part. And it's okay.

"How come you're getting along with Grandma and Grandpa, now?"

"They changed after the baby died. I could tell they felt guilty. Time heals. I don't know if I have really forgiven them, but now that I'm older, I realize those were different times.

When you were born and you looked so much like my first little baby, I had to name you Rikst. I only changed the spelling. Because you couldn't replace her."

"I understand, Mom."

Mom smiles. "Can you also understand that I couldn't tell you when you were younger?"

"Yes."

"Now that you know, I will tell Boukje. And then it's time to bring Rixt home."

"Home?" I don't understand.

"She's buried in Amsterdam and I would like to bury her here on the island.'

· 173 ·

"Does Dad know? I mean, does he mind?"

"Yes, he knows and he doesn't mind." Mom closes her eyes for a split second.

"But then the whole island will know. And you have kept your secret for so many years."

"Will you be ashamed of me?" Mom's eyes look straight at me.

"No."

"Well, then it's time I face my past." Her hands close around the swans on the music box.

"You know, Rikst," Mom reaches over and brushes my hair away from my wet face, "when you were gone the other night, and we couldn't find you, I was so afraid I'd lost you, too. And then last night I didn't think I could go through it again. I was glad I wasn't there." She puts her arm around me and presses her face against mine. "And now you're wondering why I'm holding onto the music box?"

I stay silent. There's no need to tell her that I'd found the picture already.

She opens the latch and takes out the photograph.

"There she is," she holds the photo in front of me. "You looked just like her when you were a baby. The same hair. The same eyes."

"Isn't it time you framed it?" I say softly.

Mom kisses my forehead. "You are right." We sit for a while. I look at her. She seems younger. The darkness beneath her eyes is still there, but the lines are softer. She closes the music box, but does not return the picture to its hiding place. Instead she places it on the dresser against the statue of Rixt. She smiles at me.

As she gets up to leave the room, I say, "Mom."

"Yes?"

"I'm glad you named me Rikst."

She turns off the light, closes the door.

In the dark I hold onto my paper friend, and smile.

Background Information

Ameland is one of five small islands off the coast of Friesland, in the northern Netherlands. Four small towns are scattered over the island. Today the islanders' main income comes from the tourist industry. Ameland is especially popular with German tourists. Natural gas is found near the island in the North Sea, where large drilling platforms are situated.

Legends similar to the story of Rixt appear in the folklore of many maritime nations. In all of them some poor, unfortunate or evil soul lures unsuspecting sailors into treacherous waters in order to salvage goods washed ashore from their shipwrecks.

There are many versions of the story of Rixt. In one, Rixt came from the mainland, from a town called Wierum, where she lived with her husband and son, Sjoerd. After her husband died, times were difficult for Rixt and her son. The townspeople said Rixt had made a deal with the devil. They said that at night she changed into a black cat and bewitched the children. Rixt and her son were treated like outcasts.

One night Rixt made the decision to flee to try to find a better life. They set off in a boat headed to the north. During a thunderstorm that night the boat ran aground. When morning came they realized they were stranded on an island. With the planks of their boat they built a small cottage at the edge of the island where no one else lived. They survived by taking what the sea offered to them.

When Sjoerd grew up, he left the island to sign on as a crewman on a cargo ship. For many years Rixt was alone. The loneliness slowly drove her crazy. When there were no shipwrecks, she lured ships in the night with a light or with fires on top of the dunes. Finally one day, when searching through the treasures given up by a stranded ship, she discovered the body of Sjoerd. She cried out his name and died beside him in the sand. People on the island believe that Rixt did not find peace in death, and that she can be seen wandering in the dunes during heavy storms, calling, "Sjoerd! Sjoerd!"

According to another source, Rixt had come to the island as a young girl pregnant with child. She was called a witch because she made herbal remedies for many diseases. It was said that when she found the bodies on the beach she cut off limbs in order to collect jewelry. In this version of the story Rixt died beside her son and a wave took both out to sea. During dark, windy nights you can hear a woman cry for her son.

Saint Nicholas' birthday is an event which is still celebrated in the Netherlands and Belgium. Each year, Saint Nicholas, or *Sinterklaas*, arrives on a steamship, from Spain, around the middle of November. Accompanied by his horse and black-painted helpers, he brings presents for all the children and adults. His birthday is the fifth of December and people exchange gifts during *Sinterklaas* Eve. Children in the Netherlands find no gifts under their Christmas tree.

Centuries ago when people were superstitious they practiced rituals of exorcism. One such ritual is still alive on the island of Ameland. On the evening of the fourth of December, young men between 12 and 18 years of age rule the streets. They dress-up in strange-looking outfits made of sheets. With decorated sticks and horns they clear the way of women and young children. They are the so-called 'sweepers." Anyone caught by these sweepers will get a beating.

Later on *Sinterklass* Eve the *'Sunderklazen'* arrive. *Sunderklazen* are also dressed up in costumes, which they have secretly worked on for many months. No one wants to be recognized until after midnight. These rituals are repeated on the night of December fifth as well. But now men over eighteen are the sweepers. At eight o'clock the open house parties begin. Islanders open their homes with food and drinks for every one who visits. The *Sunderklazen* go from house to house until the next morning. These days the parties are more organized, with costumed balls for young people on *Sinterklaas* Eve and for the adults the next night.